The
Sidewalk
Artist

The Sidewalk Artist

GINA BUONAGURO AND
JANICE KIRK

THOMAS DUNNE BOOKS
St. Martin's Griffin
New York

This is a work of fiction.
All of the characters, organizations, and events portrayed
in this novel are either products of the authors' imaginations
or are used fictitiously.

THOMAS DUNNE BOOKS.
An imprint of St. Martin's Press.

www.thomasdunnebooks.com
www.stmartins.com

Design by Kathryn Parise

Library of Congress Cataloging-in-Publication Data

Buonaguro, Gina.
    The sidewalk artist / Gina Buonaguro and Janice Kirk.
        p. cm.
    ISBN-13: 978-0-312-37805-9
    ISBN-10: 0-312-37805-X
    1. Women novelists—Fiction. 2. Artists—Fiction. 3. Americans—Europe—
Fiction. 4. Fiction—Authorship—Fiction. I. Title.
    PR9199.4.B86 S53 2006
    823'.92—dc22   2006045055

First St. Martin's Griffin Edition: April 2008

10 9 8 7 6 5 4 3 2 1

For Ajay, Amelia, Austin, David, and Westley

I arise from dreams of thee
In the first sweet sleep of night,
When the winds are breathing low,
And the stars are shining bright.

—Percy Bysshe Shelley, "The Indian Serenade"

I do not know whether I was then a man dreaming I was a butterfly,
or whether I am now a butterfly dreaming I am a man.

—Chuang-tzu

The Sidewalk Artist

This story begins with the rain

What truly moves Tulia is not the Eiffel Tower or Notre Dame Cathedral or any of the wonderful sights. It is the little things. A windowsill with a pot of geraniums and a glimpse of lace curtain, the way the sun glances off a puddle, the echo of her heels as she walks down a narrow cobblestone street, the taste of coffee at an outdoor café, the sound of children calling out to each other in French.

And this, this brief moment of rain, a sun shower. Sunlight spinning raindrops into gold. She raises her face to the blue sky, and the drops are cool against her skin. For her, rain has always held the memory of sadness, of loss—although she has never been able to determine why, or what it is she remembers.

The shower is over almost as soon as it starts, but its clean scent lingers in the air, and the sense of sadness is replaced by an equally mysterious sense of promise and renewal. She closes her eyes, the sun drying the raindrops like tears on her cheeks. She stores this moment close to her heart to bring out again on a gray autumn day in New York.

This sprinkle of rain like a blessing.

Smoke rings like afternoon halos

She almost missed the angels. She doesn't know how. But they are there when she opens her eyes. Cool and unruffled beneath the dappled shade of a sycamore, untouched by this short burst of rain, the angels surprise her. She would not expect them here among the vendors with their displays of T-shirts, postcards, and miniature Eiffel Towers.

The angels are enough to make her forget her aching feet and the gingko tree she just fell in love with in the botanical gardens. She has seen gingkos before but not one so magnificent, and she wishes not for the first time that her claim to a garden was more than a few pots on a concrete balcony. Not that she has the hundred years it takes to grow a tree so grand, but to start one from a little seedling would be quite a legacy.

Instead she will content herself with the pods of seeds she gathered from the garden's poppies in coral shades of pink, orange, and yellow. Already she can picture them, blooming among her cherry tomatoes and geraniums. Will she be allowed to take the seeds through customs? She wonders what harm could come if she did. Unleash a plague of poppies on New York? Hardly the thing disaster films are made of.

She loves Paris. With its wide tree-lined avenues, narrow streets of cobblestones, and parks and gardens, it is extremely walkable—and without the tall buildings of Manhattan, one can see the sky. She has come to like New York, her adopted city, but Paris has a less claustrophobic feeling—a sense that its link with the countryside has not been completely severed.

Until the sun shower, until the angels, she was looking for a bench where she could rest. She needed to decide whether to continue to the Louvre as planned or go back to the hotel and change her shoes. The cream-colored, square-heeled 1930s-style Mary Janes—an impulsive purchase the day before near the place Vendôme—were not made for hours of sightseeing. Ethan, for whom appearances are everything, would tell her to work through the pain as if she were running a marathon, but Tulia prefers comfortable shoes—and she thinks this is another difference between them that is irreconcilable.

The angels are familiar. Chins resting on plump hands, they look pensively toward an ochre-colored heaven. She stares at them again, reconsidering. Maybe *pensively* is the wrong word. Perhaps it should be *contritely*. With their mussed hair, it is possible these little angels have been up to no good.

This is no ordinary sidewalk scribbling. Rich layers of colored chalk have transformed this gray patch of pavement into a luminous masterpiece. It is the product of someone with real talent, genius perhaps, someone able to render a flat surface into something akin to flesh and blood—or in this case the divine.

His back to her, the artist kneels, adding clouds to the heavens with rapid strokes. A black beret bulging with coins sits next to the painting, and a man tosses some change into it as he walks by, his steps not even slowing. The painting is all the more fascinating for its fragility. In a few hours, the cherubs' delicate faces will be scuffed by uncaring feet, and a little rain is all it will take to return the sidewalk to drab concrete.

Tulia places a euro in the beret. She can't explain it, but it seems like the most important thing in the world that she let him know how much she admires his chalk painting. *"C'est très jolie,"* she says, addressing the thick, dark ponytail that falls just below his shoulder blades. He wears black jeans and a black shirt, both soft-looking and faded with wear. Over his shirt is a tapestry vest embroidered with a wild tangle of birds, suns, and flowers. Its colors too have mellowed with time, but it is still beautiful.

"Thank you," he replies in accented English, not falling for her French for a moment and not looking up from his work either.

"You speak English?" she asks with relief.

"I will speak anything you like," he says, turning his head slightly and addressing her new shoes.

"Except for the little French I learned in high school, I'm afraid I only speak English."

"Your French is fine," he says, and while she appreciates his desire to be kind, she also knows he is lying. Still, she thanks him as a few more coins clink into the hat.

"It's Raphael, isn't it?" she asks. "The painting, I mean."

"That is correct. And it is kind of you to stop and notice," he says without pausing in his work. His fingertips are a mélange of chalky color.

"You must've been worried when it started to rain."

"It was just a sun shower, not even enough to penetrate the leaves." He blends the colors of the clouds with the side of his hand, and they become soft and full under his touch. "I saw you," he continues. "While everyone else kept walking, you stopped. There, I said to myself, is a woman who appreciates beauty. Do you know a lot about art?"

"I wish I did," she says, feeling a little self-conscious that he'd been watching her. "But except for one art-history class, my knowledge is pretty limited." There were of course the openings she'd attended with Ethan in SoHo, the memory of which always conjures up the image of a giant ball of human hair that looked like something a very large cat coughed up.

She only recognized the angels because they've been reproduced everywhere—on coffee mugs, Christmas cards, microwave popcorn boxes, even on the sign of a pool hall near the bookstore where she works, cues clasped between chubby fingers. In fact, they have been reduced entirely to cliché. But not these angels before her, vibrant as stained glass, seemingly as fresh and inspired as the originals Raphael painted five hundred years ago.

"Are there any Raphaels in the Louvre?" she asks. "I'm going this afternoon."

"There are a few. If you sit down, I will tell you about them. I am almost finished here, and some conversation would be very welcome. Besides, those shoes look lovely on you, but they must be killing your feet."

She laughs. "They are. I was looking for a place to sit when I saw your angels." Already the sun has dried the sidewalk, and the sun shower is only a memory.

"My coat is under the tree," he says. "Spread it out and rest there. I will be done in just a moment."

She accepts his offer gladly, sinking gratefully onto the outstretched coat. It is nice to have someone to talk to. Except for the desk clerk at her little hotel on the boulevard Port-Royal, she has hardly spoken to anyone in the three days she's been in Paris.

She slips off her shoes before pulling a water bottle from her shoulder bag and taking a sip. The water is warm and tastes of plastic. She watches the artist for a moment. His back is still toward her, and apart from his long, dark hair, she has yet to get a good look at him. What she can see is a well-sculpted, olive-hued cheek, a slender frame, strong chalky hands, and the glow of the embroidered vest that is almost as fascinating as the angels. The light draws out a galaxy of moons and stars and suns before a subtle shift makes them retreat into the background and a garden of flowers and birds takes precedence. She would love such a vest, but in all the hours she has spent perusing the thrift shops and markets of the Lower East Side, she has never seen anything quite so wonderful.

Lately Ethan has been critical of her clothes—her finds, she calls them—like the antique white lace blouse and short black velvet skirt she is wearing. In the midst of one of their arguments, he told her she looked like a Dickensian waif and wasn't impressed when she told him that was exactly the look she was after. She knows he would prefer it if she dressed more like her friend Jasmine. But she is not like Jasmine, who inherited her almost-supermodel looks from her mother, a Brazilian actress. On Tulia, petite and with all the curves Ethan once professed to enjoy, designer clothes only look wrinkled. Besides, she likes her old clothes for their comfort, softness, and sense of history and doesn't care if she looks out of place among Ethan's Wall Street friends.

It occurs to her now that she could have invited Jasmine along to Paris once it became obvious she wasn't going to persuade Ethan to come. Jasmine would like the shopping, galleries, and clubs, and it would have made for a less lonely start to her trip.

She lifts her heavy brown hair from her shoulders and lets the slight breeze cool her neck. She twists her hair and draws it over her shoulder, wishing she had put it up that morning. Another lesson learned, like the shoes. Sometimes she thinks the expression about hindsight being twenty-twenty was written just for her.

To her left is the busy street. Beyond the press of cars and pedestrians she can see the cafés and buildings that mark this edge of the Latin Quarter. A man begs at a street corner. He holds out his hat and keeps his eyes lowered. A girl drops a coin into his hat, but he does not look up, nodding his thanks almost imperceptibly.

On Tulia's right, a section of the wall that borders the sidewalk is missing, perhaps under repair, a piece of yellow police tape warning pedestrians of the drop to the walkway below. Perhaps that is why the artist has chosen this spot. From her place on his coat, she sees a barge making its slow passage along the river as if reluctant to leave Paris behind. Beyond is the Cathedral of Notre-Dame, its dark Gothic beauty an almost-absurd contrast with the brightness of the day. She has already been up its towers and seen its delightfully hideous gargoyles—maybe even looked out on the very spot where she is sitting now.

The artist is still working, an occasional *merci* punctuating his silence. She is not in a hurry for him to finish. She is content simply to rest and share his shade. She leans against the base of the tree and looks up, admiring the perfection of translucent green against blue sky, when a shaft of sunlight pierces the leaves and blinds her with its brilliance.

It is an echo of the sun shower. A moment of hope and promise. But more too, she thinks—a moment of belonging. Of being completely at peace with herself and the world around her. This feeling that has eluded her so often in the past now comes to her as she sits on a stranger's coat on the edge of the Seine. The light is so strong that she is forced to close her eyes, but she savors this strange and joyous sensation of light penetrating her closed eyelids. She breathes deeply, feeling the warmth of the sun deep inside her.

When she opens her eyes at last, she finds the artist watching her, and he too gets drawn into the moment. And as seconds ago she never thought the sky could be so beautiful, now she thinks she has never seen a man so beautiful. Eyes so dark, she sees herself not so much reflected in them as lost in them—and she is powerless to look away.

It is the sound of coins falling into the hat and bouncing out on the sidewalk that breaks the spell. She looks away, feeling awkward. "I am sorry," the artist is saying. "I did not mean to make you feel uncomfortable. I was just thinking how I would like to paint you. You have very lovely eyes, you know. Blue and smoky, like the morning sky."

Even more embarrassed, she looks up just in time to catch the glance of a pedestrian. He smiles at her and drops some change into the hat.

"You see," the sidewalk artist says triumphantly. "Everyone thinks you are beautiful."

She laughs at this ridiculous conclusion but blushes all the same. "It's not me," she says, gesturing toward the chalk painting. "It's your angels."

"Nonsense. It is you. They are just a couple of foolish chalk cherubs." The artist reaches for his pack, an old green army surplus one. "Now you must eat. You must be tired from walking, and you will need strength for the Louvre." He unfastens the straps and produces from its depths a bottle of rosé, a baguette, a piece of cheese wrapped in brown paper, and, most surprising, two stemmed wineglasses. He smooths out a white linen napkin, his chalky fingers turning their makeshift tablecloth into an Impressionist's canvas.

"Can you do the *Mona Lisa?*" A very large man with a smile to match addresses them through the viewfinder of his video camera.

The artist opens the bottle with a Swiss Army knife, and the cork comes out with a satisfied pop. "You need to talk to Leonardo," he says helpfully. "He is on the other side of the bridge."

The man laughs a little uncertainly and without leaving a coin moves on, navigating his way through the camera's viewfinder.

Tulia is pondering the artist's curious response as he pours the wine. It is cold, and condensation forms on the outside of the glasses. "I am glad you are here," he says. She likes the sound of his voice, rich and polished like old wood. "I was beginning to think you were not coming."

She shifts her attention from the sound of his voice to his actual words. "I'm sorry," she says, alarmed by this colossal error. "I think you've mistaken me for someone else. I'm Tulia Rose."

He is unfazed. "Tulia Rose," he repeats as if savoring the syllables. "Tulia. Very unusual. From the Latin meaning strong rain."

"My parents are a little unusual," she explains, surprised he should know the origins of her peculiar name.

"It is a beautiful name for a beautiful woman." He holds out a glass of wine. *"Je suis très heureux de faire votre connaissance,"* he says carefully, so even she can understand.

She is even more confused now, but she takes the wine all the same. Did he mistake her for someone else? No, he couldn't have. He just said he was happy to meet her. Perhaps it was just a problem with the language. Maybe he meant to say something more like, I was beginning to think *no one* was coming, meaning he wouldn't have anyone to talk to. Still, it is a strange misunderstanding.

"Salut," he says with a smile as he touches his glass to hers.

"I'm pleased to meet you too," she says, taking a sip and thinking what a very nice smile he has. And if he is beginning to seem a bit odd, she doesn't care. She appreciates having someone to share a bottle of wine with, a chance to forget for a while why she is in Paris alone in the first place. She tries to guess the artist's age. Thirty? Forty? She can't tell, but she is sure he is older than her own twenty-five years.

"Des fleurs!" the artist exclaims, startling her out of her thoughts. "We need some flowers!" He sets down his glass on the napkin, looks up his left shirtsleeve, then his right. *"Voilà!"* he announces, looking back to her. Then, giving his sleeve a tug, he pulls out an enormous bouquet of perfectly formed red poppies.

"How on earth did you do that?" she asks, taking the proffered bouquet. The blooms are so fresh, she wouldn't be surprised if drops of dew still clung to the petals.

He shakes his head slowly. "If I told you that, *chérie,*" he says very solemnly, "it would not be magic."

She arranges the poppies in her water bottle, which she produces from her own prosaic, decidedly unmagical shoulder bag. But she draws it out with a flourish anyway. "Magic," she proclaims, earning a laugh.

The artist tears off pieces of the baguette and assembles them with the cheese that he cuts with his Swiss Army knife. He hands her one of these rather ragged sandwiches before leaning back against the base of the tree. He tells her about the Raphaels in the Louvre, and she tries to commit his explanations to memory. An occasional passerby comments on the painting. Maybe takes a picture. Drops a coin into the beret. She thinks the angels are beginning to look smug.

"So what are you doing in Paris, Tulia Rose?" he asks. She is about to say something noncommittal like "Just traveling" when he interrupts her. "No, do not tell me. Let me guess." He folds his arms and studies her, his brow furrowing. Another magic trick?

"You just broke up with your boyfriend, and you came to Europe to think," he says slowly. "Maybe even find a little romance to help you forget." She feels he is searching for a reaction, and so she looks away to the crumbs scattered on the napkin. "I am right, am I not?" he asks somewhat triumphantly as he pours them both another glass of wine. "Woman traveling alone. It is an old story."

"Wrong," she says, wondering how she gave him that impression. "It's more complicated than that." She feels some of the pleasure drain out of the afternoon. She is uncomfortable again and doesn't know how to respond. Is this a come-on? When he suggested she was looking for a little romance, was he thinking that she and he might . . .

"You have a boyfriend, but you are traveling alone?" he asks, somewhat incredulously. "Why is that, *chérie?*"

She plucks a petal from the bouquet and blows it off her palm. The chalk angels watch it float across their sky to the gray sidewalk, where it settles like a discarded valentine heart. "This is the twenty-first century," she says finally, her voice sounding petulant even to her own ears. "Women do travel alone."

"But you would have preferred if he came with you," he insists.

"I don't want to talk about it anymore." Her eyes are drawn to a couple stealing a kiss on the bank of the Seine. What can she say? A month ago she was ready to leave Ethan. She was tired of the fighting and his criticism. And she thought that breaking up was what he wanted too. Only Ethan, rather than coming right out and saying so, was icing her out, hoping she would get the hint.

But then just when she was gathering her courage to tell him that there was no point in them continuing, he had presented her with this birthday present. Six weeks in Europe. And although he can well afford it, it was a generous gift, and she was touched. Enough not to tell him what she had been thinking, enough even to ask him to come with her. Perhaps here they could relax and begin to address whatever was happening to them. But he refused, giving his imminent promotion as an excuse. If he was to make it, he couldn't take off a weekend, let alone six weeks. Besides, he said to her, what they really needed was time apart, a chance to miss each other and start anew.

"I am sorry," the artist says as the couple walks off hand in hand. "I did not mean to make you feel uncomfortable. I think I must be out of practice speaking with women." He takes a crumpled packet from his vest pocket, lights a thin black cigarette, and blows smoke rings, fragrant like incense. He offers her one as well, a peace offering, he says, and although she hasn't smoked since high school, she accepts. He lights it for her and she takes it, their fingers briefly touching.

The cigarette is strong, and although she is careful not to inhale, it still makes her light-headed. Settling against the tree again, the artist stretches out his legs. The knees of his black jeans are frayed and lightened to gray. He closes his eyes and blows another wobbly smoke ring. "Let us start again." The wispy circle of smoke hovers between them for a moment before dissolving on the breeze. "Is this your first trip to Paris?"

"Yes, and to Europe, really. My parents are English professors at the University of Pittsburgh. When I was ten, they took a sabbatical year in Cambridge, England, but that's all. I've always wanted to see more."

A sparrow hops across the ochre sky of the chalk painting and eyes their crumbs. The artist holds one out, and the bird takes it boldly from his fingers before flying into the branches above their heads. "And what do you do in life?" he asks.

"I work in a little independent bookstore in New York City." This is much easier to talk about than Ethan, and so she tells him she is the only employee at Sims & Sons other than Mr. Sims, a widower, and his identical twin sons, Tod and Tom, students in their early twenties. How after four years of working with them, she still can't tell them apart. They dress the same, wear the same little round reading glasses, and answer to either name. If a customer asks whether they are Tod or Tom, they simply answer yes. She takes another tentative puff of her cigarette, thinking how she rather misses them. She likes the bookstore, feeling at home with people who just accept and like her for herself. A big improvement over her brief stints first as a college student and later as an office temp in the firm where she met both Ethan and Jasmine. "The Simses are a bit odd," she continues, "but they're also very sweet. When my book, *Heaven on Earth,* was published, they held a launch for me."

"When your book was published?" he repeats. "Then you do not just sell books, you write them too? I am impressed."

She meant to tell him only about the bookstore—as the book, like Ethan, is something she would rather not talk about. It must be the effect of the wine, and she wonders if she will have a headache later. "I try. I haven't been feeling very inspired though. It's part of the reason I'm here. To start something new."

"What is it going to be about?"

"That's what I'm hoping to figure out on this trip."

"I think you should write about an artist. A very mysterious one who paints angels on the sidewalks of the world."

She laughs. "Why not?" she says, thinking that it doesn't seem like such a bad idea. Would he meet a young traveler from New York? It's already sounding more interesting than *Heaven on Earth.* Of course she doesn't tell the artist that the characters were modeled on her and Ethan, or that it's too bad their relationship doesn't seem to be following the course she set out in the book. Their own story, at least the last six months or so, could better be entitled *Hell on Earth.* Sometimes she wonders if the book wasn't just wishful thinking on her part. And the investment banker and the office temp lived happily ever after. The end.

An attractive woman about Tulia's age stops and asks the artist about the painting. He sits up and smiles at her. "Excuse me, *chérie,*" he says with a wink at Tulia, and she can see that the woman is already charmed. She pushes her sunglasses onto the top of her head, sweeps back her long blond hair, and, completely oblivious to Tulia's presence, smiles back. She tells him that she is from London but is in Paris studying art and has a show opening in a week. Tulia can tell the woman is already certain of her success.

Ethan is like that and for him it seems to work. It's all attitude, he tells her—she simply doesn't have the right one. She always hoped a little of his would rub off on her. She thought it had when the book was published, but from there it was all downhill.

There was the launch at Sims & Sons. Mr. Sims, Tod, and Tom were there of course, and a few people from the publishing house. Ethan arrived late, Jasmine came with a date, and a couple of regular patrons who were there only by chance stayed for a glass of champagne. Everyone bought a copy, and Tulia signed them all. The single biggest day of sales, she is sure.

There were no reviews, and the only record the book managed to break was the speed in which it found its way into the remainder bins at Barnes & Noble. Mr. Sims stubbornly keeps copies on the shelves, filed between Ayn Rand and Salman Rushdie. The embarrassing little sign he made is still there too, "Written by our very own Tulia." It is most probable that 90 percent of the sales (and that isn't saying much) were made by Mr. Sims and his sons.

The woman hands the sidewalk artist an embossed invitation to her opening and, still seemingly unaware of Tulia's presence, suggests they go for a drink. He takes the card but politely declines the offer to go out. Instead, he turns to Tulia and gives her a dazzling smile. "Thank you, but I have a friend in town." The woman doesn't miss a beat, extracting a promise that he come to her opening before saying good-bye and walking away down the quay. Before disappearing into the crush of pedestrians, she turns to give him one last wave.

Returning the wave, he tucks the invitation into the back pocket of his jeans. Tulia is pondering what he meant by *I have a friend in town* when he says to her, "I am sorry, *chérie*. Hazard of the trade. Now, where were you?"

She laughs a little ruefully. "I was just about to tell you that my book was a horrible flop and that the publisher won't even return my e-mails, but how I'm still determined to start another, despite being so discouraged I haven't been able to write a word in months."

"I will have to read this *Heaven on Earth*."

"Please don't—not that you'll ever find it. It's an overly senti-mental romance—probably best left to the dustbins of history. I never envisioned writing something like that. It's hard to explain, but I've always been convinced there's this other story inside me— I just don't know what it is yet." She stubs out her neglected ciga-rette. "Maybe it is about a sidewalk artist. I could name him after you . . ." She stops, realizing he has yet to tell her his name. She is about to ask when he interrupts.

"What is in a name?" he quotes, shaking out the napkin table-cloth.

She looks down at the angels glowing in the afternoon light and sees a scraggly signature at the bottom. *Raffaello*. "You signed the painting Raffaello. Is that your name too?"

"The English call him Raphael, but to Italians he is Raffaello," he says after a pause.

"But is it your name or just the original artist's?" she persists.

He meets her eyes. "Do you like it?"

"Raffaello," she says. Could that really be his name? Could he really have the same name as the Renaissance artist? It's possible, she supposes.

"A rose by another name would smell as sweet." Animated again, he is reciting, interrupting her thoughts. "And Tulia Rose by any other name would be just as lovely."

Although she assumes he is joking, she is flattered nonetheless and asks him if he also makes other art besides sidewalk paintings.

"I do a little of everything." He waves his hand dismissively at the chalk painting. "This is nothing. It is just copying something that has already been done. It is as easy as you copying a book. You just type the words written on the page. Simple."

It doesn't look at all simple to her. "I would love to see your original paintings."

"Who knows? Hopefully you will soon."

"Ah, but how will I know they're yours?" she asks, convinced she has him cornered, "when I don't even know your real name?"

He finishes his wine and puts down the glass next to the empty bottle. "You will know."

"You're so exasperating," she says, shaking her head. "I'm going to call you Raffaello anyway." She finishes her wine, setting her glass next to his. "Or maybe I'll just stick with Raphael, so I don't mix you up with the original painter." From now on, she'll think of the Renaissance painter by his Italian name.

"Very good," he says. "I am glad that is settled."

She has no idea if he is joking or not. More coins fall into the hat, and one rolls off and across the painting toward her. She picks it up and hands it to the artist. "I think you need a new hat . . . Raphael." Maybe it's not his real name, she thinks, but it feels right.

Taking the coin, he looks from her to the overflowing beret. "Yes, I see. But it is a small problem. Will you wait for me, *chérie?* I will only be a moment."

He gathers up the money and crosses the sidewalk to where the man she noticed earlier is still begging. She cannot hear what Raphael says, which is probably in French anyway, but the man is looking at the overflowing hat, up at the artist, back at the hat. Then it is the man's turn to talk, and Raphael helps him load the money into a canvas bag that lies next to a rolled-up blanket at the man's feet.

She is touched by this gesture on the artist's part. More than a gesture. He has given away a good day's wages. How many euros were in his hat? Fifty? One hundred? She would think a sidewalk artist would need everything he earned. Today may have been a good day, but surely there are times when he doesn't make anything. What does he do in winter, or when it rains?

When Raphael comes back, he places the hat on the sidewalk again, stopping to fix an invisible flaw on the painting before sitting down again beside her.

"That was very kind of you," she says.

"It is nothing to me," he replies. "But it will make a big difference to him. It is not hard to make people happy, and yet there is much unhappiness in the world. It is important to do what one can."

She doesn't know what to say. She gazes out over the river thinking almost absurdly that if she looks at him, she might cry. Until now she'd thought of him as charming, maybe just a little bit crazy, certainly attractive, an entertaining way to spend an otherwise lonely afternoon, but now she senses something deeper. She looks back and finds that he is watching her again—the same way he looked at her when he told her he wanted to paint her. When he told her she was beautiful. What does she see in his eyes? On the surface he is the charming sidewalk artist, full of magic tricks—but his eyes, she thinks, give away something else. Compassion, sadness, perhaps even desire.

She does not look away this time, boldly holding his gaze. She knows which way her thoughts are taking her—and wonders if his are taking him in the same direction. But then it is all moot anyway, isn't it? Ethan gave her this trip as a kind of making-up present, and she accepted, committing herself to making their relationship work. Had she refused and broken it off with Ethan, she would be free to pursue something with this man. However, then she wouldn't be here but rather begging Mr. Sims for more hours at the bookstore, just to make ends meet. And she does want it to work out with Ethan, doesn't she? Anyway, this man is a complete stranger—she isn't even sure she knows his real name. It must be the wine . . .

"I should go," she tells the artist, starting to get up.

"Wait only a few minutes more. I shall walk you as far as the Louvre." He puts out a hand and touches her arm. "I have to clean up, but if you wait, I will tell you a story."

She nods, concluding there can't be much harm in accepting his offer. She settles back on the coat.

"Once upon a time, there was an artist," he begins.

"Are you talking about yourself?"

"Perhaps," he says as he starts picking up the chalk. "He looked a lot like me—only better-looking." She likes the small lines that gather at the corners of his eyes when he smiles. "He loved life, and he savored every moment he had on earth. He tried to show that love of life in his art, and I think from time to time he was successful. He also loved women. They were life—the creators of life. Every one a goddess. That too he tried to show in his paintings.

"But he never really loved one woman. He was never, as the poets say, *in love.* Then one day, he saw her. She was in the market buying oranges. That is all. She had eyes like the dawn and the face of an angel. She looked up from the fruit stall and smiled at him, and he knew then that he knew nothing at all. That he had been blind. That he had been living only half a life. He bought her every orange in the stall. He filled her basket and carried them home for her."

Raphael pauses as if the memory has overwhelmed him, and Tulia feels a little jealous. She does not doubt this story is his own, despite his peculiar use of the third person.

"What happened?" she asks gently. "Do you . . . I mean, does *he* still love her?" Tulia already knows his answer.

"Yes," he whispers with an intensity that rather alarms her. "He has never stopped loving her. But they have been separated from each other for a very long time."

She berates herself for feeling disappointed. To think she believed the artist was flirting with her when he is obviously still in love with someone else.

"Well then, why doesn't he find her and tell her this?" she asks. "If he loves her so much."

"It is, as you said before, *chérie,* more complicated than that. There are circumstances that even he cannot control, as much as he prays . . ."

His voice trails off as he takes their napkin tablecloth, places it over the flowers, and blows on it twice. When he lifts it away, the brilliant red poppies are gone.

Drifting across rosy skies

O nly her father would give her a gift like this.
Tulia sits at a café on the Left Bank in the rosy light of
early evening while the sinking sun shimmers on the Seine, touching the roof of Notre Dame with gentle reverence. The waiter
takes away her empty soup bowl and replaces it with a salad. She
takes a bite and opens the book. *On the Trail of the Writer in Europe:
An American Woman's Pilgrimage* by Miss Mildred Mercy. Clearly
her father discovered it on one of his monthly book-buying mis-
sions, and the familiar musty odor so evocative of her childhood
rolls off the pages. It's the thought that counts, she reminds herself, as she has done over the years with so many of her father's
gifts.

In the introduction, she discovers that Miss Mercy was a retired high school English teacher from Fargo, North Dakota. In
1967, at the age of eighty, she spent the "Summer of Love" walking
in the footsteps of the writers she had spent her life teaching, and
a few she hadn't, Tulia guesses as she flips through the chapter on
Paris.

Paris is for lovers—I read that today on a young man's shirt. And certainly they are everywhere. Like in London, there are so many young people here, and they are all in love with themselves, with each other, and with life in general. I introduced myself to a group of them camping beneath a bridge by the Seine. They too were American, and they invited me to share their humble lunch of bread, cheese, and wine and were very much amused when I shared a marijuana cigarette with them. A very pleasant experience—there is much to be learned from today's young people.

Alas, Paris has not always been kind to lovers or to friends. F. Scott Fitzgerald and Ernest Hemingway met and became friends here. While their influence on each other's writings was indubitable, the friendship ended on rather bad terms. Both men too were famous for their love affairs—melodramas of near-operatic dimensions.

Amandine-Aurore-Lucile Dudevant (who, perhaps to escape such a cumbersome title, changed her name to George Sand) wooed the talented composer Frederic Chopin here in the City of Lights, but their affair was often stormy, and Frederic died of consumption soon after their breakup.

Indeed, only Gertrude Stein seems to have been successful in affairs of the heart, albeit in an unconventional union, falling in love at first sight with Alice B. Toklas. Sadly, Gertrude died in 1946 but Alice, I believe, still lives, although I do not know where. It is rumored that Alice, believing her beloved Gertrude to be immortal, has since converted to Catholicism in the hopes of being reunited with her soul mate in the afterlife.

Tulia can see why her father might have chosen this book, identifying perhaps with the author's idiosyncrasies. Not that her father would ever be so adventurous. He would never sit by a bridge and share lunch—let alone anything else—with a bunch of strangers. It was challenging enough to convince him to allow her friends to stop by their house in Pittsburgh or the old family cabin in the Poconos. But she can imagine him using *indubitable* in a sentence.

Pulling her still-empty notebook closer to her, she gingerly picks up her pen, then sets it down again, worrying that her writer's block hasn't budged. She knows this feeling all too well, not having written since the failure of *Heaven on Earth*. The first time, though, was at college.

"What happened at college?" Ethan asked her on their first date when she alluded to her failure. "I don't know," she said. "I froze." She'd been so excited to get the scholarship to such a respected writing program. It also provided an escape from the tomblike silence of her parents' house. What a shock to discover writing was as ruthless a business as any other. No one in her program seemed very interested in making friends; they saw everyone else as potential competition. It didn't seem to be about writing anymore, and at the end of her second year, after a series of incompletes and false starts, she was told not to come back.

But now, when she closes her eyes, she sees him, her first character, waiting for her. Not a sidewalk artist but an artist nonetheless. If she holds out her hand, she is almost convinced she can touch him. Strange how a chance meeting on a Paris street has given her the start of her story.

A glass-roofed tour boat glides along the river, and she recalls the feeling she had earlier that day—that she was part of the fabric of Paris. Sitting with the sidewalk artist under the tree with his angels, sipping wine as he blew smoke rings.

She wishes she could thank him in person, but she has lost that opportunity. After he finished packing his bag, he walked her over the bridge (the one under which Miss Mercy had shared lunch with those young people?), across the Île de la Cité, and along the Right Bank to the giant glass pyramids by the entrance to the Louvre.

The whole distance she went over his strange story. A story that seemed to say that while he loved someone else, they were no longer together. And a story she was beginning to think meant he was available. Why else would he have told her so much? As they approached the ticket booth, he even seemed to be waiting for an invitation, waiting for *something*—or so she thinks in retrospect. She pondered asking him to join her but decided against it. He was attractive and she was lonely and afraid of what could happen. Ethan was trying to make their relationship work, and she had to respect that. So not knowing what else to do, she stuck out her hand instead. They parted ways with a good old American handshake.

Still, she did feel a small knot of regret as she watched him stroll away in the direction of the place de la Concorde. And as she wandered the halls of the Louvre in stockinged feet, her shoes dangling from her fingertips, her thoughts kept returning to his receding back, the suns and flowers of his vest illuminated in the sunshine.

The Raffaello paintings were housed in the Grand Gallery. Several studies of saints and dragons; *La Belle Jardinière,* in which a graceful Madonna sits in a garden with the Christ child and baby John the Baptist; an almost-regal portrait of Baldassare Castiglione, who was, as Raphael had told her over lunch, a good friend of the painter.

But she was especially interested in *Self-Portrait with His Fencing Master,* a picture of two men, one of whom, so the label said, is thought to be Raffaello himself. The portrait of Raffaello wasn't quite what she expected, and she realized she was comparing it to the sidewalk artist. The eyes in the painting though, were remarkably like Raphael's in color and shape but without their depth— that sense of looking into the night sky. He was, she thinks, *très beau.* In English, *beautiful* is an adjective usually reserved for women, but it is the only word she feels comes close to describing him. *Good-looking, handsome,* God forbid, *cute*—all are inadequate.

It really is too bad she will never see him again. She feels a touch of sadness and recognizes how much she liked him. Here was someone comfortable in his own skin, someone who seemed to know what he wanted out of his time here on earth. She could sense a warmth, a genuine interest in other people, a caring for how they felt, and a generosity too.

Thank you, she thinks. I don't know who you are, but I'll always be grateful to you.

The waiter brings her a café au lait and a candle for her table, the flame casting a warm glow over the new white page in front of her. Finally ready to start, she picks up her pen and writes her first words in months.

And there you were

He did not travel these streets often, only when in need of a new shirt, as he was now. Children, their dirty faces pinched and undernourished, watched him with varying degrees of suspicion and curiosity, some going so far as to follow him from a distance.

This part of Roma reminded him of his younger days spent in Firenze, for everyone here was engaged in the production of cloth. Spinning, dyeing, weaving, sewing. Over his head, clotheslines held freshly dyed skeins of wool like so many triumphant banners, the only bright colors that made their way into these otherwise dark, filthy streets. Women sat weaving or spinning on rough benches against the drab buildings, for while the light was bad here in the street, it was a hundred times worse in their almost windowless houses. Under whose auspices this industry functioned in Roma, though, he did not know.

He stopped in front of the pitiful home of the seamstress. The door was firmly closed, and the woman was not seated outside. Sure that his trip had been wasted, he nonetheless knocked on the battered entrance. He was about to leave when the door opened, revealing a little girl with knotted hair and a grimy face. Dirt, mothers believed, protected children from the plague. The girl boldly looked him up and down, silently taking in his fine clothes and polished boots. He could hear a baby wailing in the darkness behind her.

"Is your mother home?" he asked kindly. He assumed she was the daughter of the seamstress. He did not know how these women kept track of so many offspring. The houses and streets overflowed with children, until, despite the layers of protective dirt, the next round of plague thinned their numbers once again.

"She isn't here. She's gone to the market." The girl pointed down the street, then abruptly shut the door. He stepped back, and the small circle of children who had edged closer to him scattered like mice. He did not want to make this trip again anytime soon, and he questioned his insistence on patronizing this woman directly instead of shopping at Roma's fashionable merchants. But he knew he would continue to do so, aware that the merchants paid these women barely enough to starve on. As this woman's sister had once been his servant, there was a more personal connection too. She had died in childbirth at his house, unwed, and no father stepped forward to claim the child. So he himself had brought the baby to the seamstress, only to learn later that it had died within a few days. Since then, he had felt an urge to assist the woman who had counted on her sister's wages to help support her family.

He strode toward the market. A woman in the next doorway held a baby at each breast, one dark-haired like herself, the other so fair her curls were almost white. He wondered offhandedly whose bastard child the woman was wet-nursing. A slightly older child crouched in the street in front of her, poking with a stick at what appeared to be a dead rat.

A group of men were gathered around a table, no doubt engaged in a game of dice. He shook his head. While the women in this quarter seemed to be forever working, it appeared the men were forever idle.

The narrow street opened onto a large piazza, and here the farmers had set up their rickety stalls. More light streamed through, but despite the abundance of fresh produce heaped onto the carts that lined the piazza's northern edge, an overwhelming smell of decay permeated the area. On the other side stood the animals, the snorting oxen and braying donkeys that had drawn the carts from the countryside. In the center was a well, around which the farmers traded news and gossip, while at the stalls their shrewd wives hawked their wares, their high-pitched voices competing with the squawking fowl stacked behind them in wooden crates. A small group of boys, their feet blackened with the filth of the streets, gathered near the opening of the piazza. They watched the women attentively, waiting for one to become momentarily distracted by a customer or a husband so that they might grab a piece of fruit and run.

After he gave each of these boys a small coin, they scuttled out of the piazza and down a dark alley as fast as if they had just robbed him. He walked along the line of stalls, inspecting each suspicious face that stared back at him, but he did not see the familiar pointed features of the seamstress. He resigned himself to the fact that this trip was wasted after all and that he would have to return another day.

He glanced up at the buildings that leaned precariously into the street as if at any moment they might topple and crush everyone in the piazza. A woman at an open window lowered the bodice of her dress with one hand, revealing her breast while beckoning to him with her other hand. He looked away quickly. How could a single city contain so much wealth and beauty in one quarter and so much poverty and shame in others?

He was about to leave the market in disgust and return by the way he came when he heard her voice.

Forever after he was to think how quickly and unexpectedly everything could change, like the way the casual addition of a different color could irrevocably alter the hue of a pigment. And whenever he was to think that he might never have met her—that he might have turned away a moment too soon or that his favorite shirt might not have been ruined after His Holiness's feast last week, that he might never have come here at all—he almost died with the anguish. Her voice, so musical in this cacophony of shrill voices, wailing babies, screeching geese, floated to him like a wondrous hymn. Pure and clean like water in a brook rolling over pebbles.

He stopped instantly, oblivious to the chaos around him, and searched for the source of this heavenly sound.

And there she was. Only a stall away, attempting to bargain with an old woman over oranges. They were beautiful oranges, fragrant and ripe, reddish in color, a luxury no one could really contemplate in this market where buyers could afford only what would keep them from starving.

"Please, signora," she said. "I have no more money, but I can give you this in exchange." She held out a small handkerchief with an embroidered edge. "It is very good lace."

The market woman grabbed the tiny square of cloth, so white in her dirty hand, and gave it a cursory glance. "I don't want it," she replied harshly, thrusting it back.

The young woman took it and was about to speak again when she stopped. She seemed aware of his eyes on her and slowly turned toward him. Their eyes met, and she smiled at him, so openly and freely, an exchange between equals. Her beauty made his breath catch. Eyes like the dawn and the face of an angel . . .

To: Tulia
From: Ethan
Subject: **I almost forgot**

Tulia:

I almost forgot to water the geraniums and tomatoes on the balcony. But I remembered them last night, and you will be happy to hear they are alive and well. Hope you're having a good time. I am, and I'm stuck in New York working these long hours. I also hope you are coming to see what a great idea it was for you to go to Europe on your own. How does the saying go, "Familiarity breeds contempt"? Not that I feel contempt, but you know what I mean. Anyway, cheers! I'm off to dinner and the clubs with some of the gang from work.

Ethan ☻

Reply

Dear Ethan:

Do you remember the night we met? It was that dreadful office party Jasmine dragged me to just after I started with the firm. I felt so out of place in that sea of suits and Vidal Sassoon hair, and being only an office temp, everybody just ignored me. Except you. You swept me off my feet that night. First the wonderful dinner (I remember thinking that meal would have cost me a week's salary), then the ride on the Staten Island ferry—you couldn't believe I'd never done it before. It was cool on the deck, and you gave me your jacket, and all the time the skyscrapers were glittering against the night sky like the Milky Way. "It's all ours," you said. It sounded a bit sappy at the time, but there was nothing sappy about your kisses, and it was all we could do to wait until your apartment door closed behind us before tearing off each other's clothes. I never did make it home that weekend, and on Monday Jasmine took great delight in noting I had on the same dress I was wearing Friday. She told me there wasn't a single woman in the office who wasn't green with envy.

Perhaps we could get back some of this magic. Can't you make a little time for us? Couldn't you meet me for a long weekend in Amsterdam? We may have some problems now, but for the most part it's been a good four years.

I miss you.

Tulia xxxx

Delete

Ethan:

Sounds like you're doing fine. Paris is lovely. Yesterday I sat by the Seine and started my new novel. It's off to a good start. So maybe my coming alone was a good idea after all. Thanks for remembering to water the plants.

Au revoir,

Tulia

Send

The poor little angels

I t is the sad remains of the angels that push Tulia over the edge.
She sits down under the tree and lets the tears spill over. Less
than twenty-four hours after its creation, the sidewalk painting is
ruined. Someone has drawn eyeglasses on the cherubs and cigarettes between their fingers, while French obscenities are scrawled
in cartoon bubbles above their tousled heads.

She has retraced her steps here, hoping to see the sidewalk
artist, for she doesn't want to be alone right now. She feels shocked
and hurt by Ethan's message, and yes, angry too. Just when she was
thinking she and Ethan might finally be heading in the right direction, he sends her this flippant message. He was the one who said
they needed time apart to miss each other, and though she didn't
agree with his method, she was happy that he seemed to want to
patch things up. Yet he doesn't appear to be missing her at all. In
fact he seems quite pleased about all the fun he's having while she's
out of town. Not that she expects him to sit around and brood—
that certainly isn't Ethan's way. But what about a little compassion,
a little sense that he's giving his own idea a chance to work? He

didn't even end his e-mail, *Love, Ethan*. Instead, he signed off with a happy face. He usually hates that kind of thing. Too cutesy.

As for the e-mail she didn't send—well, she's not even sure how much she meant it. It felt hollow even as she wrote it, as if it was what she was supposed to write, how she was supposed to feel. When you're on the verge of breaking up, you're supposed to remind each other of all the good times, right? And they certainly did have their share.

After her failure at school, being with Ethan was exhilarating—she felt like she could do anything, even write again. And if the result was an overly sentimental romance—well, at least it was something. And she was, after all, in love. Ethan was all too happy to help her. He set up a timetable, helped her work out a plot outline, and found an agent through a contact of his sister's. Really, it was his book as much as hers. He was unfazed by her problems at school, living instead by those sentiments expressed on inspirational office posters. *There are no obstacles, only opportunities*—that sort of thing. He kept his own list of goals and set up his daily life to achieve them. Train every day for the marathon, become managing director at one of the largest investment-banking firms in New York by thirty, find a girl, sweep her off her feet, turn her into a best-selling author.

Only the last part didn't work, and as *Heaven on Earth* slid from obscurity into oblivion, he became more detached. They barely saw each other all winter, and they hadn't had sex in weeks. He was working twelve to fourteen hours a day, going out to the clubs every evening with his colleagues, and running ten miles each morning. She was asleep when he came in and asleep when he left in the morning, only going out to work at the bookstore or to wander aimlessly around Greenwich Village as usual. Ethan was spending free weekends at the boss's vacation house in Vermont. In the past, she had gone with him, inviting along Jasmine, who as a mere secretary was delighted to be a part of the firm's inner circle. But this year he has yet to ask Tulia to join him, and she suspects he now finds her embarrassing. He had wanted to make her into a so-phisticated New York writer as if she was just another line item on his CV, like his standing in the Boston Marathon. But when he failed, he lost interest. It was *My Fair Lady* gone awry.

So in the end, she went with the safe, vague reply, the one that most matched his tone. What else could she do? She doesn't even know what she wants. She has thought of talking to Jasmine, but Jasmine isn't much of an expert on long-term relationships. "The minute I find myself picking up someone else's socks," Jasmine has said more than once, "I'm out of there."

It is all the worse because she checked her e-mail looking for reassurance. After the great start on her next book, she went back to her hotel and fell asleep, only to be awakened by a dream. She doesn't think a name even exists for the type of dream she had. Nightmares are frightening, but this was different. What she ex-perienced was more like falling into an abyss. And yet she has no idea what the dream was about. Just the awareness that something or someone was there, encompassed in fog, trying to reveal itself. But whatever it was, her subconscious didn't want to know, and it was her own cries that woke her.

She dries her tears on her lacy sleeve and is looking again at the poor angels when something in the painting's bottom corner catches her eye. More words are scribbled above the signature. Not wanting to contribute any further to the painting's ruin, she stands and steps around it, bending down in order to read the words, writ-ten in the same hand as the signature. *The Tour Eiffel is truly a tall on Tuesdays.* It is a nonsensical message, but the *a* on the end of the word *truly* catches her attention. Take out the *r* and it could be her own name. Spelled differently, but sounding the same.

Can this message be for her? Is Raphael at the Eiffel Tower, maybe working on a new sidewalk painting? She stands for a few minutes on the spot where they lunched the day before. When a poppy petal blows across the spoiled painting, she becomes sure he wrote this message for her.

She smiles. Of course she'll go. Today is Tuesday, it's her last day in Paris, and she planned on going to the Eiffel Tower anyway.

On the day balloons filled
the sky

He is there. Not in the park that surrounds the tower but up on the observation deck. Tulia sees him the moment she gets off the elevator. Smiling, he leans against the rail, arms crossed over his chest. His back is to the sun, and his body is framed with light. He wears his hair loose, the dark waves drifting over his shoulders. His clothes are the same as the day before, the hues in the embroidered vest glowing warmly in the sun. Everything about the sidewalk artist, she decides, is warm. So different from Ethan in his expensive gray Italian suits and cool arm's-length demeanor. She smiles back, feeling better already.

"Right on time," Raphael says.

"How can I be on time?" she asks. "You didn't even know I was coming."

"I knew you would get my message."

"But how did you know I'd go back there? Let alone understand your message?" None of this makes any sense to her.

"How could I not know?"

Unable to think of a good reason, she shakes her head and laughs. "Well, at least now I get to thank you."

"Thank me? For what?"

"For inspiring me. I started writing my new novel yesterday. So *merci,* Raphael."

"Is it about a sidewalk artist who paints angels?"

Remembering his coy answer when she asked how she would recognize his paintings, she decides to be equally mysterious. Besides, she is a little hesitant about admitting how much his story affected her. Let alone that it is his face that floats before her as she writes, even though she is using the real Raffaello as her main character. "Sorry," she says. "It's too soon."

He doesn't seem offended. "Ah, well. I will find out when it is a best-seller, and then I can brag to everyone that I knew you."

She murmurs her doubts about such an outcome, noticing at the same time that they are alone on the tower. The elevator hasn't let out a single tourist since she arrived, and not a single one remains.

"You are right," he says when she mentions this. "I am sure it is a very rare event to have the whole tower to oneself." Draping his arm around her shoulder, he gestures with his free arm, taking the whole of Paris into his embrace. "I love seeing the city from the sky. The last time I was up here it was night and I watched a storm move across the city. Ahead of it came the wind, so strong I thought it would sweep me away. Then the lightning, long ragged forks that lit the sky purple. And at last the rain, as if the very heavens had opened . . ."

He continues, but she scarcely hears his words. She is too distracted by his body touching hers. The weight of his arm across her shoulder, the whisper of his sleeve against her neck. And the scent of him, a blend of his fragrant cigarettes and something she can only describe as summer. If he kissed her now, what would she do?

But instead he stops talking and pulls away from her, leaning back against the railing again, arms crossed. Only this time he is not smiling. "What about—I am sorry, I do not know his name—your boyfriend?" he asks as if he knows what she is thinking.

"His name is Ethan," she says. "And I don't know. I got an e-mail from him this morning. I don't think he misses me very much."

"Then he is a fool."

"Thank you," she says. "I'll take that as a compliment." It is breezy on the tower, and the blue cornflowers on her Indian-cotton skirt swirl around her ankles. "Anyway, we're having some problems, but we're supposed to be working them out."

"Do you still love him?" he asks quietly.

Looking over his shoulder at the sky, the same blue as her skirt, she doesn't know how to answer. She loved him once. And the tone of his e-mail wouldn't have hurt so much if she didn't love him, right? But then, if she still loved him, why is she wondering what it would be like to kiss this man?

"Perhaps you believe too much in your book," he says when she fails to answer. " 'And they lived happily ever after.' That is how it ends, right?"

"That's just a story," she says defensively, though he is closer to the truth than she cares to admit. "I know the difference between fantasy and reality."

"What I mean, *chérie*," he says earnestly, "is that there is not just one happy ending. There are several. Maybe you and Ethan will make it. And maybe you will not. Maybe your happy ending with Ethan already happened, when you first fell in love. And maybe the sad end to your story is in fact the start of something else wonderful. A whole new story waiting to be written." He brushes the windblown hair out of her eyes. "Anyway, it is much better this way."

"Why's that?"

"It is much more interesting. If there was only one happy ending, life would get a little dull. Sort of like heaven."

"Heaven?" she asks, perplexed.

"Yes, heaven. The ultimate happy ending. But you have to admit, it would become boring just floating around all day on a cloud being happy."

She laughs and rolls her eyes.

"What?" he says, sounding a little surprised. "You wrote a book called *Heaven on Earth,* and yet you do not believe in heaven?"

She doesn't know if he is being serious or not. "Not really. I guess I'm willing to accept there could be some sort of higher power out there. But I can't imagine that he or she or it is all that interested in us." She sometimes wonders if this committed agnosticism is the only thing she has in common with her parents.

"Why do you say that?"

"There's so much misery in the world. Wars, famine, global warming. We're making such a mess of things. Surely any god would want to distance itself from us."

"Yes, but there are those who are committed to saving this world. I like to think God looks down, sees those people, and says, very good, keep it up, because one day you will succeed."

"You are a true optimist, Raphael." Her tone is one of admiration, though she herself feels less hopeful about the course history is taking. It is the sort of debate that echoes through the bookstore, although she and the Simses are usually in agreement.

"I understand your fears, but there is reason for hope too. The world holds much love and beauty, though at times it seems scarce." He pauses for a moment, then smiles. "I am sorry, I did not mean to tell you a sermon—if that is how you say it in English. Why do we not instead talk about the Louvre? Did you see the Raffaellos?"

"Yes, and they were wonderful," she says, suddenly remembering his angels. "But I'm afraid your sidewalk painting is ruined."

He is unperturbed. "It would not be sidewalk art if it lasted forever. Part of its appeal is its fleeting nature, its temporary beauty, so different from paintings and frescoes. One only hopes it lives on in someone's memory."

"I'll never forget it," she says. Or you, she adds to herself.

"That is most kind of you," he says softly, and she is unsure for a moment whether she has spoken her thoughts out loud. "But I hope you did not go to the Louvre just for the Raffaellos," he goes on.

"Mostly."

"You at least saw the *Mona Lisa,* I hope."

"Me and a million other tourists," she says with a bit of new-found art snobbery.

"There is good reason why it is so popular. It is a brilliant portrait that had a tremendous influence on every painter who saw it. Including Raffaello."

"Did it?" she asks, feeling both curious and slightly chastised.

"Yes. Raffaello thought that da Vinci portrayed in the *Mona Lisa* the ideal woman, or at least da Vinci's ideal—something Raffaello felt he never accomplished in his own work."

She wants to ask Raphael who *his* ideal woman is—the woman with the oranges? But already he is moving on to a new topic. "What did you think of the self-portrait, the one with the fencing master?" he asks.

"I don't know. It wasn't what I expected."

"It is the beard. He never liked that beard. The self-portrait at the Uffizi in Firenze is much more flattering. And the one in *The School of Athens* too, but you will have to go to Roma for that."

"Maybe it is the beard," she says, studying the man beside her. This is what she imagines her character to look like. But with a beard the Raphael before her *could* look something like the Raffaello in the portrait. Same Mediterranean dark looks. And those eyes . . . "I guess I'll have to content myself with the self-portraits in the book I bought at the Louvre gift shop. I'm afraid Italy isn't on this trip."

"That is too bad. You would like Italy. And with your hair and complexion, you might even have some Italian blood."

"English, I think, though I don't know much about my family history." Her parents rarely talked about her grandparents, all long dead, and with no uncles, aunts, or cousins, holidays were often very lonely affairs, no different from any other day of quiet reading and reflection. In fact, unless she has children someday, she is the last of the Roses.

"You will have to go sometime. I think you would feel at home there." He takes her arm and they walk around the perimeter of the tower. He names for her the bridges over the Seine and points out Sacré-Coeur Basilica on top of Montmartre and Napoleon's burial place, the Hôtel des Invalides, its gold dome glinting in the sun. When they have made a full circle back to the elevators, she has an instinctive feeling their meeting is over. But she doesn't want a repeat of yesterday outside the Louvre. Still, it is hard to know what to ask. Does she want him to romance her on the streets of Paris for the rest of the day? To fly to Amsterdam with her? A European fling to make her feel better? This morning she almost asked Ethan to meet her in Holland, and now she doesn't want to leave this stranger. "Will you come to the Luxembourg Gardens with me?" she asks finally. Whatever happens, she will deal with the guilt later.

"It is too soon for you, *chérie,*" he says gently. "You need to make up your mind about Ethan. You do not want to do anything you will regret."

She looks away from him and back over the city, feeling not only disappointed but also like an idiot. Did she misread the situation that much? "That's all right," she says, attempting to salvage her pride. "I leave tomorrow for Amsterdam anyway."

"I know," he says. It is a simple affirmation, although she hasn't told him before where she is going.

This is ridiculous, she thinks. She only met him yesterday. And yesterday he so much as told her he was in love with someone else. Which is pretty much the only thing she really knows about him. All the rest she has imagined—a solitary celibate existence, painting and mourning the loss of his love. Until she came along and helped him forget . . . Maybe she doesn't know the difference between fantasy and reality after all. But then, given the mixed messages he has been sending, she shouldn't be too hard on herself.

"It was nice to meet you, Raphael." And while she knows she will remember him, she hopes the intense way he is looking at her means he will miss her a little too. Maybe he's as confused about his feelings as she is about hers. Perhaps if the timing had been different . . .

"And you too, *chérie*." He slowly releases her hand, and before she steps into the elevator, he kisses her gently on both cheeks. When she turns to wave one last time, she sees him, not standing where she left him, but balancing on the narrow railing of the tower—almost four hundred feet above the ground! "Good-bye, Tulia," he calls. Then, to her disbelief, he does a cartwheel along the railing. His upside-down body is outlined briefly against the sun before his feet land safely again on the observation deck.

"Raphael!" she chides him, laughing with relief as the elevator doors close. It all happened so quickly. She cannot quite believe what she has seen. A man standing on his hands, hundreds of feet above the ground. Fearless. Laughing. Showing off. For her.

She disembarks at the bottom and notices the long line of tourists waiting to go up. Where did they all come from? She wanders to the edge of the park and looks back up at the observation deck. Of course she cannot see him. The tower is too high, and she is too far away.

Loneliness seeps back into her spirit, and she is about to turn and leave when the sky fills with hundreds of red balloons. Released from the top of the tower, the breeze carries them upward and outward like a joyous burst of fireworks. She stands there, unconscious of time, watching until the last one is only a dot in the heavens.

He filled the sky with balloons just for her. Her last magic show.

And then you were gone

And there she was. Eyes like the dawn and the face of an angel.
All the squalor around him was forgotten. But just as he
stepped forward to address her, a cloud suddenly passed over her smile. She
seemed confused and embarrassed and looked away quickly.

"Never mind," she said to the woman hurriedly. "Keep your oranges."
She was about to turn away when the old woman spoke again.

"I'll take that," she rasped, pointing to the young woman's hair with a
gnarled finger.

"This?" she asked in surprise, her hand flying up to touch a golden comb
that gleamed in her dark brown hair. He couldn't help but compare her to
the other women in the piazza. Her clean white muslin dress, her almost
luxurious red shawl, the comb inlaid with three red stones that she covered
protectively with a soft fine hand. Such a contrast to the work-worn
women. And yet she had no money for an orange.

Her hand still on her hair, she hesitated and looked longingly at the
tempting orange pyramid. "No," she said finally, "it was my mother's." He
heard a note of despair in her voice. She started to walk away, letting go of

44

the comb to lift the hem of her dress so as to avoid the animal waste and garbage.

"Wait!" he called. He almost leapt forward, catching her arm with his hand. *Anything, dear God, just let me speak to her.* She looked down at his hand on her sleeve, but he did not give her time to react. "How much for them all?" he asked the old woman urgently, not able to take his eyes from the young woman's face. He was so close he could smell her hair, sweet like a meadow after the rain.

"All of them?" the old woman croaked.

"Every last one," he said. The young woman looked up with puzzled wonderment from his hand on her sleeve to his face. He took in the long dark lashes, the soft blue of her eyes, the flush of her cheek, the perfect curve of her lovely red mouth.

Ah, for one kiss . . .

The old woman named a price he knew to be exorbitant even for oranges, but he did not care. He handed over the money with his free hand. He was forced to release the young woman's arm in order to load her empty basket but was rewarded with her smile. And when her silence turned to laughter again, he felt like the sun had exploded inside him. He filled her basket and opened shawl and was forced to give the last two oranges to a little urchin who was watching them with wide eyes from around the corner of the cart. Like the boys with the money, she too scampered off with the prize.

The young woman began to lead him away from the stall and out of the piazza. "I hope you do not live too far from here," he said with a small smile, his arms laden. He did not let on that in truth he would have followed her to the ends of the earth.

She led him down twisted streets no more wholesome than the ones they had just left. He followed behind with the basket and waited while she pushed open a gate into a narrow alley between two sagging houses. At the end of this alley was the door to a cottage. She opened that too, and he followed her inside.

He closed the door and stood in the dark for a moment while she unfastened the shutters on a window in the rear, the sun weakly filling the cottage's only room. Next to a small fireplace a narrow bed pressed against the wall, and a bench with a washbasin and a pail of water leaned against the wall opposite. A makeshift shelf over the bench held a plate, a bowl, cups, a couple of earthenware jugs, and a pile of folded linen. Next to the bed hung a dress similar to the one she was wearing, and under the window stood a rude table and chair. The room was simple but clean, and the scrubbed plank floor gleamed darkly in the watery light.

A jug overflowing with wild roses stood on the table in front of the window. He approached it to set down his heavy load and was astonished to discover beyond the window a tiny, tangled garden. Surrounded by crumbling stone walls, it was her very own retreat from the squalor of this quarter. "Those walls are Roman," he noted with amazement. It was the first thing he had said since they left the market. He could glimpse the roofs of the houses on the other side of the wall, but no other window had a view of this miniature Eden.

He set down the basket, while she let the oranges roll from her shawl onto the bed, one falling with a soft thud to the floor. She opened the door next to the window, and the room filled with light. The air was redolent with mint and roses, and he followed her out into the garden. Along the crumbling walls trailed wild roses of the softest pink. A stone path led around the perimeter, and in the middle grew a fragrant mix of herbs. A single brilliant red poppy nodded among them.

He was so moved by this small patch of beauty, so wild but so utterly perfect, that he could not speak for a moment. He looked at the woman beside him, framed by the roses on the wall behind her, and thought he could not bear so much beauty at once.

She smiled gently. "Let me bring you some wine. To thank you for your gift of oranges."

"This is all the thanks I need," he said, making a sweep of the garden with his outstretched arm. But she went into the house again and returned *with two mismatched cups full of wine. She led him to a stone bench, and they sat together, only inches between them. He took a sip of the wine. It was surprisingly good.*

She was silent, and he was so full of questions for her. But uncharacteristically for one so used to making easy conversation, he did not know where to begin, and so he was quiet too. He was sure she wasn't married; the tiny room and single bed suggested she lived alone. But how did she come to have this cottage and garden? How did she live? Again he looked at the delicate fingers cupping her wine, so different from the roughened hands of the women who worked at menial tasks. How did she support herself? Was she the mistress of a merchant or nobleman? If so, he was already jealous. He did not even let himself contemplate that she might be a prostitute.

"Look," she whispered, pointing to a hummingbird that hovered among the flowers.

"How did it find its way here?" he asked, full of wonder.

"A happy accident, I suppose."

Like myself, he thought. The bird had broken through their silence. "I should introduce myself. I am Raffaello Sanzio."

"The painter?" Clearly curious, she took her eyes from the bird and looked at him.

"You have heard of me?" he asked. He saw himself reflected back in her eyes and thought how happy he would be to drown in their light.

"Everybody has heard of Raffaello Sanzio, the pope's favorite artist." She turned away and watched the hummingbird as it darted between blooms.

"You flatter me. What about Michelangelo? Surely he is better known."

"Perhaps for his temper," she said lightly.

He laughed. In awe as he was of Michelangelo's achievements—especially the ceiling of the Sistine Chapel—Raffaello was nonetheless no admirer of his person, and the two of them had an uneasy relationship at best. The man was egotistical and jealous. Unable to see that they all influenced one another's work, Michelangelo was convinced that everyone stole their ideas from him. But while his lack of graciousness was common knowledge among his colleagues, Raffaello wondered how this woman came to know of the man's reputation.

"You are interested in art then?"

"Very much," she said. "My uncle once took me with him to Chigi's palazzo, where I saw your work."

"I am only one of many contributors." To think their paths could have crossed at his good friend Agostino Chigi's house, where he had spent so many hours!

"Yes, but the nymph Galatea, being pulled on her shell by dolphins, that is yours."

"True," he assented.

"And the frescoes in the loggia. Unfortunately, I fear they do not exhibit the same grace as the lovely Galatea."

He was impressed and flattered by her knowledge. "You are a very honest critic, and an astute one. The paintings in the loggia are the work of my students, and while I have great respect for them, I realize they were not quite ready for such a task." Emboldened by the wine and the comfortable conversation, he dared to satisfy at least some of his curiosity. "How is it that you live here?"

She looked at him, and whereas a moment ago she was relaxed and smiling, she now seemed tense. "It is too long a story," she said finally.

"I would like to hear it," he said gently. He was more curious than ever, and he longed to touch her and bring the smile back to her lips. But instead she shook her head slowly.

His cup was empty, and somewhere a clock chimed the hours. He remembered then that he was to meet with Pope Leo over a commission, but if she asked him to stay, not even an audience with God himself could make him leave her or her garden.

"You need more wine," she said, holding out her hand for his cup. "Then you must tell me what it is like to be the most popular painter in Roma."

At the return of her radiant smile, His Holiness was forgotten. He almost jumped to his feet. "Let me, please," he said, reaching for her cup. She relinquished it, and their fingers brushed.

He entered the house, turning in the doorway to see her still sitting on the bench, a rose raised to her face as she drank in its fragrance. He set the cups on the table in front of the window, went to the shelf, and took down the jug of wine.

The orange that had rolled from the bed rested where it had fallen. He picked it up and placed it on the table. That was when he noticed the tiny stack of cheap paper weighted with a smooth pebble. The script was flowing and feminine, her writing, he was sure. He traced the curve of the opening letter with the tip of his finger as reverently as if it were the curve of her breast. And while he knew he should have looked away, he could not help but read the opening lines.

But he could not stop there. Slowly, he set the jug on the table and removed the pebble. He felt the poetry reach for his very soul. The wine forgotten, he turned over the top page. To take mere words and use them to express the very divine in the world. What he tried to do with paint every day and failed so miserably at, this woman had accomplished with pen and ink.

Scarcely remembering to breathe, he moved aside the top sheet and started to read the second page. He did not hear her enter, and when she spoke he looked up, startled.

"What are you doing?" she cried. She lunged for the papers and knocked over the jug. It rolled unharmed into the oranges. He surrendered the papers, and she backed away from him, the pages held against her breast. Her blue eyes filled with angry tears.

He could still feel her heat from where she had grazed against him. He was out of his depth. He felt her anger and something else he could not name. Please, God, he prayed silently and urgently. Do not let this happen. "I am sorry," he said, pleading with her. "I should not have read it. But it was so beautiful. Once I started, I could not stop." He took a step toward her, but she backed away against the opened door.

He stood still again. The light streaming through the door touched her brow and one cheek, the rest of her face in shadow. He could not stop the artist inside himself. Oh, to paint her, he thought. And that was the problem. Too many thoughts competing. He wanted her to stop looking at him like that. Wanted to kiss away the desperation in her face, assure her that he would love her and take care of her. Wanted to tell her that her words were the most sublime he had ever read.

If only he had taken a moment to think, but he had not. The weakness of his sex perhaps. He was too worried that she was slipping away from him, and so he took another step toward her, catching her in his arms, the pages floating to the floor like autumn leaves.

What did I expect? he asked himself a thousand times after he found himself in the rutted street outside her gate. He had acted like a boor, and she had reacted accordingly. His cheek still stung from where she had slapped him, and he touched it with his hand. "I am not a whore!" she had exclaimed. He had let her go immediately, ashamed. "You think I can be bought with oranges?" she had said, her voice like ice. He had protested, but she had only opened the door and told him to leave.

Looking at the battered gate, he never would have imagined that it led to such a small slice of paradise. A hidden garden and the most beautiful woman he had ever met. And when he finally turned and walked away, he realized he did not even know her name.

Trying to fly

*U*n *billet pour Amsterdam, s'il vous plaît.*"

Tulia's French doesn't fool the clerk. "Just sold out," she responds in English. She is chewing gum. "You missed the last seat by one minute."

Tulia looks behind her at the crowded, noisy terminal of the Charles de Gaulle Airport as if to spot the culprit who took her ticket. Damn, she thinks as she looks at her watch. 9:05 A.M. She's early too. But then she should have booked ahead. She reserved her hotel in Amsterdam; it was pretty stupid not to book her flight as well. Good thing Ethan isn't with her. This type of sloppy planning on her part drives him insane. As it is, she can hear his admonishments from across the Atlantic.

She pushes Ethan from her mind and tries to focus on the situation. A long line snakes behind her, and she can feel impatient eyes boring into her back, wishing she would fall through the floor. "When's the next flight?"

"One thirty-five. But it's sold out too. There's an international potato conference in Amsterdam."

Her writer's imagination piqued, she tries to picture planeloads of potato farmers dressed in overalls flying from Paris to Amsterdam. She can't. Where did all these potato farmers come from? Surely they don't live in Paris? Perhaps she has misheard the clerk. She wants to ask her, "Did you say *potato conference?*" but the woman is peering over her head, anxiously scanning the line that is lengthening by the moment. "When's the next one?" Tulia asks instead.

"Seven-ten P.M. Better get your ticket now." The clerk snaps her gum.

"I don't know," she says slowly. She can't bear the thought of spending the whole day in the airport. And to go all the way back into the city—it's too exhausting. She has said her good-byes to Paris and she just wants to be sitting on the plane. She didn't sleep well, afraid the awful dream might return, not to mention trying to sort out her feelings about Ethan as well as the sidewalk artist.

"Look, why don't you come back when you know what you want to do."

"No!" Tulia nearly shouts. She has to get out of here. "What's the next available flight?"

"Seven-ten," the clerk snaps.

"No, not to Amsterdam. To anywhere." She will lose the deposit on her hotel, but that's better than waiting.

Now the clerk is looking at her as if she has lost her mind. "Well, anywhere in Europe, that is," Tulia adds hurriedly. She doesn't want to end up somewhere in Australia or Asia. Then it comes to her. "Italy!" The sidewalk artist thought she would like Italy. She can see there the paintings he mentioned, the self-portrait and *The School of Athens.* Other Raffaellos too—Italy is where he lived, after all. And she can do research and make progress on her book.

The clerk rolls her eyes. "Are you sure?"

Tulia nods, excited by this change of plans.

"Where in Italy?"

Where did he say those paintings were? She can't remember. She wonders if the clerk might know but can't bear any more exasperated looks. "I don't know, anywhere."

She is not spared another infuriated glare before the clerk checks her computer. "Venice," she says. "The plane leaves in thirty minutes."

"I'll take it," Tulia says as she places her credit card and passport on the ticket counter. She'll worry about the locations of the paintings later. Besides, she thinks, further justifying her change in plans, Venice has canals just like Amsterdam, and there won't be as many potato farmers. And given that no one will be waiting for her at the other end, does it really matter what flight she gets on?

She races to the gate, the last person to board, and the door closes with a clunk as she slides into her seat. Her seatmate, an older woman with silvery hair and wearing a brown tweed suit, reminds Tulia of a slightly less rumpled version of her mother. But this woman is one thing her own mother is not—motherly. She introduces herself as Doris and insists Tulia take the window seat so she can see Paris from the air. She then offers her peppermints, which she instructs her to chew if her ears pop. And when the flight attendant comes around with his cart, she insists that Tulia take her snack as well as Tulia's own.

Tulia wonders if Doris is like this with everyone or if she looks particularly in need of mothering. This last-minute change of plans with its subsequent dash for the plane has left her feeling even more disheveled than usual, and so she attempts to push her hair back into the morning's makeshift bun. She wipes her face with the warm wet towel the flight attendant passes to her with a pair of tongs, then tries to sponge the coffee spill off her jeans, the consequence of a rushed breakfast.

Doris is talkative, another way in which she differs from Tulia's mother. Already Tulia has learned she is from Dublin and on her way to Venice to meet her husband, an engineer overseeing the rebuilding of a canal. Normally he flies home for the weekends, but as this is their fortieth wedding anniversary, he is treating her to a few days in Venice. They have two children and four grandchildren, and she carries a photo album in her purse of their recent vacation in Interlaken, Switzerland. Tulia dutifully looks at the pictures and, after listening to a litany of praises for her family, has to conclude that the similarities between Doris and her mother pretty much begin and end with the silvery hair and brown tweed suit.

Nevertheless, she decides to call her mother as soon as she arrives in Venice to let her know about her new itinerary. She should be telling Ethan too but doesn't want to. Guilt over the sidewalk artist perhaps? Her mother, however, won't ask questions. Tulia can hear her now, that slightly vacant "That's nice, dear," the response to almost everything Tulia says.

There is also the rest of her trip to worry about. She will cancel her hotel in Amsterdam, but what about the other reservations? Most of her time is supposed to be spent in England. While her plans are somewhat haphazard, she does have a bus tour booked. Like Miss Mercy, she has planned to spend some time "on the trail of the writer." The Lake District for Wordsworth, the moors for the Brontë sisters, London for Virginia Woolf. The rest is to be spent writing at a bed-and-breakfast in Yorkshire, hopefully inspired by her travels. Should she cancel this too? Or should she see how Venice goes? One thing is certain though. She has to be back in London in five weeks to catch her flight home. Already the thought fills her with dread.

Doris stows her photo album in her vast purse and, drawing out a pair of cloth eyeshades, prepares to take a nap. She asks the flight attendant for blankets and hands one to Tulia, who spreads it over her lap and looks out the window.

They are over the Alps now, but whether they are French, Swiss, or Italian, she can't say. A few snowy peaks push through, little islands in a milky sea. Then the clouds part and she can see down into a valley where a river winds like silver ribbon. Below the snow line, tiny toy houses sprinkle steep green slopes.

"Glorious, aren't they?" Doris says, leaning over her to get a glimpse of the peaks.

"I love mountains," Tulia agrees. "My family used to have a cabin in the Poconos in Pennsylvania—though they're only hills compared to these." She doesn't tell Doris how the cabin was passed down from her grandfather to her father, and how she always dreamed it would be hers one day. A place for her to go and write, her cat, Charlotte, on her lap. There was an old kitchen garden that had gone wild, a jungle of mint, horseradish, black-eyed Susans, and catnip. And the lake that turned damask rose in the setting sun, the loons with a call that could break one's heart, and the leaves that whispered secrets in the breeze. In her dream there was also a man, perhaps even children, and she would sit by the lake and watch them play. Take their pictures and keep a photo album in her purse like Doris.

From the Poconos to Manhattan. How far she has strayed from her dreams. Ethan loves the city and would sooner move to Mars than the Poconos, would never consider having children, and is allergic to cats. As the clouds close over the mountains again, Tulia leans back and closes her eyes. Doris, her mouth slightly open, snores quietly beside her. She asks herself why she is still finding it difficult to let Ethan go. Yes, it is hard to accept that one is no longer loved, and his indifference to her over the past months has hurt. But she knows there is a harsher reason for not leaving: she was scared and still is. Where would she go? How would she support herself? Her salary at the bookstore is far from adequate, and given that she still doesn't have a college degree, the likelihood of getting a decent-paying job is pretty low.

Can she return to college? Possibly, but she is now pretty wary of writing programs. She could declare a different major, but she can't imagine what that would be—she's always wanted to be a writer. And even if she can get into another writing program, how would she pay for the tuition? She squandered the scholarship with all those bad grades.

Pittsburgh? It may come to that, although it's the last place she wants to go. After she left college, her mother did suggest she return home, but Tulia suspected the invitation was extended more out of a sense of duty than a genuine desire to have her back. It was a suspicion reinforced by the news that they had sold the cabin in the Poconos and put down her cat. (She was getting old, dear, her mother said. Maybe, but it would have been nice to be consulted.) Besides, with her high school friends settled in different cities, she would be awfully lonely.

If she stayed with Ethan, these difficult situations could be avoided, but she can't even begin to contemplate that she would be doing so only because he supports her. What a soul-destroying thought. But the fact is, although she insists on contributing her meager income to covering the co-op fees, Ethan does handle the mortgage and all the other big bills.

She knows now the decision she faces. If she and Ethan can get back the good times they used to have, if she can honestly say again that she loves him, then of course she'll stay. But if she can't do that, she'll have to leave. She won't stay with a man she doesn't love, or who doesn't love her, only for financial security. She will have to summon her courage and move out—probably return to Pittsburgh and live with her parents, as distasteful as that would be for all of them, until she figures out what to do next.

The pilot announces over the loudspeaker that they are preparing to descend. It is partly cloudy and 72 degrees in Venice. Doris wakes up, puts away her eyeshades, and offers Tulia another peppermint. Tulia pops it into her mouth as the plane drops through the clouds—and she has a flash of other clouds, painted in chalk on a sidewalk in Paris. *You have lovely eyes,* he said. *Like the morning sky.*

Lost in a maze of water
and stone

A gentle early morning breeze flutters the silk curtains at the open French doors, and Tulia can hear the rhythmical lap of water against a gondola as it passes beneath her balcony. She has already become accustomed to these sounds, to these peaceful sights, which would be so strange back in the usual chaos of New York. *You would feel at home in Italy,* the sidewalk artist had said.

She has been here for three days, her time divided between exploring the city and working on her new book. Each morning she sits at the antique desk in her luxurious hotel room looking out over the quiet canal. Ethan, she thinks, would be impressed by her choice of accommodations—elegant and indulgent.

She takes a sip of her steaming cappuccino and a bite of fresh pastry, the breakfast she has delivered each morning, and flips to the section on Venice in Miss Mercy's book. Quite taken aback by the hourly rate charged by gondoliers, the author goes on at some length about her unsuccessful attempt to talk one down in price. Tulia thinks he must have been a very courageous gondolier to take on Miss Mercy.

Once safely installed in a gondola, though, Miss Mercy turns literary again. Henry James, Thomas Mann, Lord Byron—all were writers in love with this city. Robert Browning died here, and Miss Mercy spends many pages on the turbulent relationship he had with his son Pen. But it is the sad story of George Eliot that most captures Tulia's imagination.

I have taken here as my lodgings the Hotel de l'Europa, where Mary Ann Evans, better known to the world as novelist George Eliot, spent her honeymoon. It is perhaps a macabre homage on my part, as the hotel was to play a significant role in the newly wedded couple's swift dissolution.

George's new husband was a man twenty years her junior, an American banker by the name of J. W. Cross. It was by all appearances a marriage of love, so we can perhaps conclude that the groom did not share Henry James's rather unkind observation that his bride, George, was "magnificently ugly" or "deliciously hideous."

But what was it, then, that drove Mr. Cross to take such drastic measures? Was it the heat? The sun? A sudden fit of madness, as he professed? Or some darker reason buried deep in his psyche? Had the couple chosen an alternate venue for their honeymoon—Paris, Rome, New York— would the outcome have been quite different? Would they have lived long and happily together, the world enriched with more novels under her singular nom de plume? Alas, we shall never know the answer to that any more than we will ever know what possessed the young Mr. Cross to hurl himself from his hotel window into the fetid waters of the Grand Canal.

Fortunately for Mr. Cross, he was rescued by passing gondoliers and taken to Verona. He made a full recovery there and lived to the respectable age of eighty-four. But there was no one to rescue the poor bride. She returned to England and died six months later of an apparent kidney infection, although I am inclined to believe that disappointment must have played a hand in her demise.

Tulia thinks Miss Mercy would have made a great writer of Gothic romances. She has already formed an image of her: Dr. Scholl shoes, support stockings, and an enormous handbag stuffed with tissues, notebooks, knitting needles, yarn, and a big bottle of liver pills.

Putting the book away, Tulia picks up the volume on Raffaello she purchased in the Louvre. There were shelves of books on Michelangelo and Leonardo but few on Raffaello. She chose the one with the most reproductions of his works. The cherubs of the sidewalk painting, she learned, are only a small detail of a larger work, *The Sistine Madonna,* one of the numerous renderings of the Virgin Mary the artist did on commission. But while the book is thorough in its discussion of paintings, displayed on dozens of colored plates, there is a disappointing lack of detail about the painter himself. The author apologizes for this but says in her defense that very little is known, right down to his date of birth. The inscription on his tomb in the Pantheon in Rome reads that he died on his birthday, Good Friday, April 6, 1520, at precisely thirty-seven years old. But it was apparently customary in Renaissance times to use feast and saint days to mark birthdays. So was Raffaello born on April 6, 1483, or on Good Friday, which in that year fell on March 28?

Tulia likes the Good Friday version of the story, and so she has marked in her notebook: *Raffaello Sanzio—born Good Friday 1483 in Urbino. Died Good Friday 1520 in Rome.*

She reviews her notes.

Born to Giovanni Sanzio, painter in the humanistic court of Urbino. Mother died when he was 8. Studied with his father, who died when Raffaello was eleven. Was sent to Perugia to apprentice with Perugino, among the most famed painters at that time. Learned his style so well that art historians have difficulty telling their paintings

*from that era apart. Did his first independent commission before he was
20. Spent his early twenties in Florence painting commissions for
wealthy families and studying with Leonardo, Michelangelo, and others.
Painted dozens of Madonnas. Moved to Rome at age twenty-five to
work for Pope Julius II and then Pope Leo X in the Vatican. Helped re-
design St. Peter's Basilica. Painted* The School of Athens, *which de-
picted ancient philosophers and scholars exchanging ideas. Catalogued
Rome's ancient ruins. Was famed for his numerous romantic liaisons, especially with his models. By all accounts was a charming and generous man
with a multitude of friends. Died of a fever at age thirty-seven before
completing his final and perhaps greatest work,* The Transfiguration.

She carefully studies the plate for *The School of Athens,* easily lo-
cating Raffaello's self-portrait among the figures. Beardless, he
does indeed fit the character of her imagination, so heavily influenced by her memory of the sidewalk artist. She wonders if she
should go to Rome to see it, but she is so happy in Venice she
doesn't want to leave quite yet.

Then she flips to the last few pages of text, noting the plans for
Raffaello's arranged marriage to Maria Bibbiena, a relative of a
member of the pope's court. But she died before the engagement
was finalized. And even though she is buried with Raffaello in the
Pantheon, it is unclear whether he mourned her passing or even
ever met her.

He did have a favorite lover though—the model for the portrait *La Fornarina,* known in English as *The Baker's Daughter.* Dark
hair wrapped in a scarf, she holds one hand against a naked breast,
her navel just visible through the sheer fabric draped over her
voluptuous body.

Tulia contemplates the painting while finishing her breakfast.
Is this the woman for whom the Raffaello of her novel will buy
oranges? For while she is now committed to using the historical

Renaissance master as the hero of her book, she is also determined to incorporate her original inspiration, the story told by the sidewalk artist. But while the baker's daughter is undoubtedly lovely, she doesn't seem right, doesn't inspire her as much as her own vision does. She closes the book and places her dishes on the silver tray to be put outside her door. Enough for one morning. She will work out this dilemma later. The day promises to be gorgeous, and the city calls out to be explored.

She gave up on her guidebook the day after she arrived, choosing instead aimless wandering, not minding if she became lost for hours at a stretch in this maze of water and stone. She meanders down a side street so narrow that the crooked buildings almost touch above her head. Finding this enchanting, she leans against the cool stone to gaze at the sliver of sky. Inevitably, she runs into a dead end and finds herself standing at the edge of a canal, no place to go without a boat. She admires the reflections in the quiet water before retracing her steps, only to discover that she has taken a wrong turn and is somewhere else new and wonderful.

She eventually makes her way to the Piazza San Marco and its famed basilica, resting inside until the church's size and majesty start to overwhelm her. She leaves feeling somehow smaller, more human, ready to believe in something much greater than herself. Outside, she studies the basilica, its gold roof shining in the sun, crowned with domes and spires, a perfect blend of Eastern and Western architecture. Oblivious to the angels hovering above, the bronze horses over the entrance shake their manes. The piazza teems with tourists. Yet even they are outnumbered by the well-fed but never-sated pigeons swirling fearlessly around the square, awaiting handouts of birdseed bought from vendors.

Passing an Internet café, she forces herself to keep walking, emerging eventually in a peaceful park. She should send Ethan a message so he knows she hasn't gone missing, but she has been resisting the urge to check her e-mail, hoping to give him the chance to miss her.

She is so busy going over the possible messages he could have sent that she almost doesn't see it. A fresh chalk painting, its colors still vibrant and unsmudged. She does not recognize the subject and so does not know whether it is a reproduction or an original: a young man, his hands folded in prayer, looking up in awe at an angel fluttering close overhead, while at his side a dog barks at the strange apparition.

This park is an odd spot for a sidewalk painting. Not a heavily trafficked area. The artist could not expect to make much money. Unless, of course, money was not the primary objective. Perhaps it was made for pleasure, either his own or that of the occasional passerby like herself. A gift from the artist. Whoever that might be.

She sits on a bench by the painting and can't help but think of the sidewalk artist. This painting could have been his. Angels, maybe not by Raffaello, yet angels all the same. But her sidewalk artist is in France. She remembers his eyes, warm like a summer sky at night. But melancholy too—that faraway look when he told her about the woman with the oranges. Tulia wishes that every time she thought about Ethan, the sidewalk artist didn't intrude on her thoughts.

Eventually she finds her way back to her hotel and, stretching out on the bed, wonders what Ethan is doing. It is still late afternoon in New York. He is probably making plans to go out to eat with some colleagues before returning to the office for another late night. He is probably working even harder than usual with her out of town, she thinks as she drifts off to sleep.

But almost immediately, she is awake again. She sits bolt upright in bed and, cowering against the headboard, looks wildly around the dark room. Reaching for the bedside lamp, she knocks over her water glass, which falls to the floor with a thump. She fumbles with the lamp, almost knocking it over too before she is finally able to turn it on.

Light floods the room, but no one is there. The French doors are open, a slight breeze ruffling the curtains. Her books sit undisturbed on the desk. It is so peaceful and quiet, yet her breath still comes in short gasps, and she is almost crying. She leans over the side of the bed and picks up the fallen glass with a shaking hand. There is a dark stain where the water has soaked into the red carpet.

She almost drops the glass. That dream again! She tries frantically to identify what it is that disturbs her so much. There is nothing inherently frightening, at least that she can see—just this terrible feeling that something or someone is there in the mist, a ghostly image struggling to reveal itself, to free itself from the dark. But she fights against this knowledge, forcing herself awake before she can identify what it is. It is as if the dream is trying to tell her something, something she doesn't want to know. Or is she afraid of being drawn into that poisonous-looking mist? Is that why she awakes gasping for air?

She wishes Ethan was with her. She looks at the clock on her bedside table. It is only eight o'clock in New York. Ethan would be either still in his office or out somewhere having dinner. She could call his cell phone but can't quite bring herself to do it. It sounds pathetic to call someone all the way across the ocean just because she's had a nightmare. But nonetheless, she resolves to find an Internet café first thing in the morning. Everything will be okay.

To: Tulia
From: Ethan
Subject: Re: **I almost forgot**

Tulia:

Hope you're having a good time and glad to hear you're writing again. Things are fine here. Jasmine came by on Saturday night. She forgot you were in Europe. As it turns out, she needed some help with her investment portfolio and stayed for dinner. I'm helping her set up her new computer this weekend. Then we're going to the Yankees game—she scored some great tickets. She says hello and to send her a postcard.

Weather is nice here. I'm watering the geraniums and tomatoes on the balcony faithfully.

Can't think of anything else new.

Ethan ☻

Reply

ETHAN:

SOUNDS LIKE THE GERANIUMS AND TOMATOES ARE THE ONLY THING YOU'RE BEING FAITHFUL TO. LIKE HELL YOU WANTED ME TO COME HERE TO WORK ON MY WRITING—YOU WANTED TO GET ME OUT OF TOWN SO YOU COULD GET MY FRIEND IN BED! OR DID YOU TWO HAVE THIS PLANNED ALL ALONG? BECAUSE I DON'T BUY THAT SHE FORGOT I WAS GOING TO EUROPE. AND I WON'T BE SENDING HER A POSTCARD EITHER. YOU JERK, ETHAN. MAKE SURE YOU'RE GONE BY

THE TIME I GET BACK—BECAUSE I NEVER WANT
TO SEE YOU OR JASMINE AGAIN.

TULIA

(AND WHAT'S WITH THE STUPID HAPPY FACE?)

Delete

Dear Ethan:

I guess I'm not completely surprised by your e-mail. But I
am disappointed. I thought we were trying to work things out.
I guess it's hard to find time to miss me when Jasmine's in our
bed all the time. . . .

Delete

Ethan:

Glad you're well. Thanks again for watering the plants and
say hi to Jasmine for me. The weather is nice here too. I
skipped Amsterdam and came to Venice instead with someone
I met in Paris. Having a great time!!

Ciao, Tulia ☺

Send

Angels rest in quiet places

There it is. The original of the sidewalk painting in the park near the Piazza San Marco. The fluttering angel, the young man watching in amazement, his dog barking in alarm. "And here we have the church's namesake, Raffaele." Tulia moves in closer to listen to a woman addressing a small group of tourists. "One of the seven archangels who has seen the face of God."

She does not know what brought her here, to this almost-empty stucco church in a tranquil section of the city. The Chiesa dell'Angelo Raffaele. Dwarfing the neighboring houses, the church's square twin towers loom over the canal. She does not know how long she walked, oblivious for the first time since her arrival to the wonders around her. She could only picture Ethan and Jasmine. Talking, laughing, making love. She should have seen this coming. No wonder he was no longer asking her to go away on weekends; he was probably spending them with Jasmine. Ethan wasn't just embarrassed by her, he was clearly bored with her too. And he didn't even have the decency to tell her to her face.

"I was sure the church was still closed for renovations," the guide continues. "And so it is quite a thrill for me to see this cycle again. Painted by the artist Gianantonio Guardi, they depict the story of Tobias. One day, the angel Raffaele appears in disguise to Tobias, and together they travel in search of a cure for Tobias's blind father, Tobit."

Tulia tries to reason with herself, to be logical. How can she be angry with Ethan when she herself was perfectly ready for a fling? It was only because Raphael thought she needed to sort out her feelings about Ethan that nothing happened. How ironic, given that Ethan is having an affair of his own.

It's time she accepted that their relationship is limping to its pitiful end. But for now she'll play his little game, which is why she wrote that she was traveling with someone to Italy, hoping he might read *someone* as male. Ethan needs to think he's not the only one having fun. And at the very least, this fictitious someone is giving her the shot of confidence she needs right now to save face.

"Along the way, they meet Sarah," the guide is saying. "It is love at first sight for Tobias and Sarah, but first Sarah must be exorcised of a demon that has killed her suitors before."

Tulia only half listens. Although he is still in Paris, she should admit to herself she was envisioning the sidewalk artist when she wrote *someone*. She keeps seeing him wreathed by sunlight on the Eiffel Tower, doing a cartwheel on the railing just for her. She feels a fresh wave of resentment toward Ethan. If it wasn't for him, maybe she would be with Raphael right now. Instead, she'll never see him again.

"Raffaele tells Sarah how to drive off the demon, and the couple are wed," the tour guide notes, indicating the painting that depicts a wedding feast. She turns to the final painting. "At last they return to Tobit's home, and Raffaele tells Tobias how to cure the old man's blindness. He then reveals himself as an archangel. See how in this panel the angel's wings are spread protectively over the family? The tale ends here—happily—for everyone. From this story, the angel Raffaele earns many titles. Among others, he is the patron saint of happy meetings, single people, travelers, and good health. In short," she finishes with a smile, "happy endings."

Happy endings. That day on the Eiffel Tower, Raphael said there wasn't just one happy ending. Maybe he was right. Maybe this ending with Ethan is really the start of something new and exciting, something she can't even anticipate with someone she hasn't even met yet.

The tour group is about to move on, peering into darkened corners on their way to the exit. A couple lights a candle. The guide is answering a question. As another visitor opens the door to leave, a shaft of late-morning sun streams down and lights up the guide's auburn hair.

Tulia freezes. She is so overwhelmed by a sense of déjà vu that she feels dizzy. This woman is evoking something. What is it? She frantically searches her memory. The woman turns slightly toward her, and something glints in her hair. It is a comb, a gold one, reflecting the sun's light. Again Tulia is struck by the feeling of déjà vu. But now she knows where she has seen this before. Her dream! She saw the comb in her dream, a gold one with three red stones, she is sure of it. Not on this woman but on another. A woman with dark hair. She can see her now again—not her face, her back was to her—but she can envision her sitting at a table. She seems to be writing something . . .

How can this be? The woman in her dream is the same as the woman in her new book. And yet, until now, try as she might, she could not recall the details of the dream. But the details are already there in her book, right down to the comb with the red gems. Has her book been giving her these nightmares? But why? There's nothing at all disturbing about her story, so why does she wake up from the dream feeling so much anguish?

But at least she is remembering. Is this a good thing? In her dream she is so conscious of not wanting to know, of forcing herself awake to avoid whatever it is trying to tell her, and yet bits of it are coming out in her story. This is all so incomprehensible. And while last night she was able to comfort herself with thoughts of Ethan, today she knows she will have to confront this dream on her own.

She looks around. She is alone in the silent church. Unaware of the chaos she so innocently created in Tulia, the guide with the comb is gone.

Tulia is about to leave when she sees a rack of cards, prayers to be said to the angel Raffaele. Taking one, she raises her eyes to the paintings. This angel guiding by the hand. She could use someone like Raffaele to watch over her and give her strength. But all she has is the memory of a sidewalk artist with the name of an angel.

Saying prayers

Glorious Archangel Raffaele. Protector of travelers, Healer of the sick in both body and soul, Arranger of happy meetings, and Orchestrater of happy endings. As you guided Tobias and Sarah toward happiness, guide me too, that I may share in the bounty of joy that you long to bestow on those who love you. Spread your Luminous Wings, O Gentle Raffaele. Encircle me in their gossamer folds and comfort me. For my heart is heavy with confusion and longs for the healing balm of your love. Sing to me the Ancient Songs of Angels, Raffaele. Soothe away the loneliness with a gentle lullaby and fill my heart with the blissful whisper of hope that I may love again. Bless my tears with gentle fingers and with prudent words so that I may go forward in the knowledge of your grace. Liberate me, Great Raffaele. Free me from this fear and darkness and guide me safely toward the sun that I may live once again in the light. I beseech thee humbly.

My loving Raffaele

Singing songs too ancient to remember

He is standing by the bridge that crosses the Rio dell'Angelo Raffaele, and although Tulia recognizes him immediately, she can't quite believe it. She thinks for a moment that she has gone crazy, that she is hallucinating, conjuring him up with her thoughts. She stares down the narrow street that runs along the side of the church, not knowing what to do, when he smiles broadly at her. There is no doubt now that he is real, and for at least a moment, everything else is forgotten.

"Raphael!" she calls out as she hurries toward him. "I can't believe you're here! I'm not even supposed to be in Venice. I was to go to Amsterdam, but the plane was sold out." He is still smiling, and she knows he is pleased to see her too.

She pushes away the hair that has fallen over her eyes and points to the church. "I was just in the Angelo Raffaele looking at the paintings. The name made me think of you." She doesn't say she has been thinking of him ever since she left Paris. "And here you are . . . Raffaele—the angel, that is," she says, showing off her new knowledge, "is the patron saint of happy meetings. Fitting, I think."

She looks at him more closely now, comparing him with the angel of the paintings in the church. Both are beautiful, but her Raphael wears a striped shirt instead of wings and fans his face with a straw hat. "You look like a gondolier," she says.

He points over the edge of the low brick wall to a gondola moored on the canal. "May I take you for a ride, signorina?" He dons his hat with a flourish and holds his hand out to her, leading her down the stone steps to the boat. His large, rough hand envelops her small one, and even though the gondola rocks, she feels safe. She settles into the tapestry cushions that line the seats.

"This is the way to see Venezia," he says, taking his position standing in the boat's stern and pushing them off into the canal.

"Where did you get the gondola?"

"From a gondola store, of course."

"Will you ever give me a straight answer?" she asks, shaking her head.

He laughs. "Maybe when you stop asking so many questions." Skillfully guiding the gondola along the canal, he greets in Italian a gondolier passing the other way. So now she has even more questions. How he became an expert gondolier, why he speaks Italian. In Paris she assumed he was French, but now she isn't even sure of this. She contemplates asking him his nationality but decides against it. She should insist on an answer, but given the morning she's just had, she just wants to relax and let the moment carry her. Her hand touches something cool among the cushions, and she pulls out a bottle of white wine. "Is this for you or your passengers?"

"You do not think I would drink and drive?" he asks playfully. "There is a glass down there for you too."

She pours the wine, feeling like a queen as she watches Venice glide by from her nest of cushions. "I saw a sidewalk painting yesterday. It's a copy of the one in the church of the Angelo Raffaele. Did you do it?"

It is a question but not one he seems to mind. "Did you like it?"

"Yes, very much." First the cherubs and then this angel, she thinks. For Raphael it really must be as easy as retyping a famous story.

"Tell me," he says, his oar slicing confidently through the water. "What took you to the Angelo Raffaele? It is not a place many tourists find."

"I guess you could say I stumbled across it. I needed a place to think." He does not ask her more, but she plunges on anyway. "I had an e-mail from my boyfriend," she says. "Or rather, my ex-boyfriend."

"So that story has taken a turn for the worse." He guides the gondola around a corner, taking them into a narrow canal. Resplendent with purple blooms like bunches of grapes, fragrant wisteria spills over a crumbling brick wall. No other boats are in sight, no other tourists either, and without these physical reminders of the twenty-first century, it feels as though they could be anywhere in time, just the two of them, alone in this magical place.

"I'm pretty sure Ethan is having an affair with my friend." Although she doesn't want to get her hopes up, she can't help but wonder if this news will change Raphael's mind about being with her.

He directs the gondola under a stone bridge, the darkness cool against her face. "I am very sorry, *cara.*"

"And I've been having these dreams too," she continues. "Well, two of them, or maybe a recurring one. One in Paris and now one in Venice."

There is a heartbeat of silence as they slide once more into daylight. "It disturbs you, *cara.*"

She nods. "It's so strange. I wake up feeling terrible, but I can't remember anything—just a desolate void. Until now. I was sitting in the church, and suddenly I recalled something. Not much, just a few details. Nothing frightening, and yet I was scared all the same.

And what's more, I've somehow been incorporating the dream into my book, even though until now I didn't think I remembered anything."

"You would not be the first artist inspired by dreams."

"I'd rather not be one of them," she says. "This dream is far too disturbing. Besides, I'm not sure if the dream is inspiring my book or whether the book is giving me the dream. After all, it started after I began writing."

He stops rowing to let another gondola pass. "All I know, *cara,* is that dreams often have something to tell us. But please do not be frightened." He says it so reassuringly that she already feels better. "Now will you tell me what your story is about?" he asks, resuming his paddling.

"Sorry, Raphael. I've told you a lot, but I'm still not going to tell you that."

He doesn't seem too disappointed. "Then what about your other story, the one in New York?"

"Well, we had a lot of problems, but we were supposedly trying to work on them. And I was just starting to believe that my coming alone on this trip was a good idea. But I guess he only wanted me out of the way so he and my friend could spend time alone. So he's made my decision a lot easier." However, she can't help but feel like a fool too. It certainly was easier to think about doing the leaving rather than being left.

"You are not a fool, you know," he says, and she again has the feeling she had in Paris, that he is reading her thoughts. "You put your trust in someone, and he broke it. It would hurt anyone. But do not worry, *cara.* You are stronger than you believe."

She thinks back to the paintings in the Church of the Angelo Raffaele. Patron saint of travelers, of healing, of happy meetings, of single people. She has never been religious, but the prayer card she found in the church comforts her. She needs a guardian angel to lead her to a new happy ending. *If there was only one happy ending, life would get a little dull. Sort of like heaven.* She smiles. Perhaps she has the next best thing to a guardian angel—a slightly crazy sidewalk artist who pops up everywhere she goes with a bottle of wine. And sometimes a gondola.

"What brings on that lovely smile?" he asks.

"Would you be my guardian angel, Raphael?" She wonders if she might be a little drunk.

"I can be whatever you like," he says solemnly.

He sings to her then. Not "O Sole Mio," which she always imagined gondoliers singing, but something she has never heard before, in a language she does not recognize.

The sun finds its way between the shuttered palazzi, turning the water emerald. Time has dropped away and left them alone together. She catches again the scent of blossoming wisteria, listens to Raphael's singing and the gentle touch of the water against his oar. She realizes now that what she feels for this man is more than just physical attraction. And whereas in Paris she was hoping for just a fling, now she is free to consider something more.

Utterly content, she savors this moment and muses on what life would be like with the sidewalk artist. Very different from life with Ethan, she knows that much.

Her eyes begin to close and she thinks maybe she will sleep for just a minute. It is siesta time, after all. She is settling further into the cushions when she sees Raphael's vest, the one he wore in Paris. She pulls it out from under the cushions to study more closely the embroidered birds and flowers when a battered wallet drops out of the pocket.

Suddenly wide awake, she covers it with one hand and looks up at Raphael. He has stopped singing and is talking with an approaching gondolier.

She feels on the brink of a discovery. No longer content to call him Raphael, she picks up the wallet and opens it. No identity papers, no passport, no birth certificate, no driver's license or credit cards. Just a few euros, a couple of American dollars, and some change. If he is carrying the secret to his identity, it's not here. Disappointed, she folds the wallet up and is putting it back into the vest pocket when she glimpses something in a side compartment. Glancing up again at Raphael, who is still engrossed in conversation, she slips it out.

A plane ticket. That's all. No name appears on it—that part has been torn away, whether accidentally or on purpose, she can't tell. She is about to replace it when she looks at it again. A plane ticket from Paris to Amsterdam. Dated the day she left France. 9:04 A.M.

The last ticket to Amsterdam. The one that should have been hers.

She stares at it. She told Raphael in Paris she was going to Amsterdam, but it seems he had different plans for her. Or does the ticket indicate he was planning to follow her there? Either way, it means their meeting in Venice is no coincidence. Is she dealing with some sort of sophisticated stalker? God only knows who he really is.

She looks up, shielding her eyes from the midday sun. They are stopped alongside the other gondola, and Raphael is speaking to his colleague in rapid Italian, one arm gesturing to the sky. Moments ago she would have been charmed, as moments ago she was ready to consider something serious with him. But this ticket changes all that. Until now she considered him eccentric. Maybe a little crazy, but not in a dangerous way. Now she feels betrayed, manipulated, scared, and even a little stupid. Stupid and naïve to have trusted this man who won't even tell her his real name.

I thought it was the end

He overslept and would have slept longer if it had not been for the persistent knocking on the heavy door of his studio. He called out, "Who is there?" remembering as he did so that he had arranged for her to come and sit for him. She called back her name, and he told her he would soon be with her.

Sitting up, he felt a throbbing pain behind his eyes. His throat too was parched, and he reached for the dipper in the pail of water on the table beside his narrow bed. This illness was no mystery, for an empty jug of wine sat on the table, a cup beside it.

He unsteadily rose to his feet, still dressed in the clothes from the day before, his shirt pressed into a thousand wrinkles, and went to the windows. He folded back the shutters, and sunlight streamed into the room, its rays piercing his brain like arrows. But the air at least was fresh that morning, and he inhaled deeply. Through lines of laundered linens stretched across the street, he glimpsed a cart laden with straw. There was another knock at the door, timid this time, and he turned from the window.

"Please forgive me," he said as he opened the door. "I overslept."

"Are you unwell?" she asked, laying one plump hand upon his sleeve.

"*I fear it is my own fault,*" *he said.* "*It will pass.*" *He moved away from her, and her hand stayed poised on the air for a moment before returning slowly to her side. He went and drank again from the dipper, the water tasting of wood.*

She looked uncertain standing there, not sure whether she should venture farther into the room. She knows it has changed, he thought, for I did not acknowledge her touch. He busied himself with placing the easel, watching as she looked around the room at the canvases that leaned against the water-stained walls, the table with its neat row of brushes and jars of pigments. Her eyes went to the unmade bed before modestly dropping to the floor as if to study the direction of the wood grain. It is as if she is seeing the room for the first time, he thought. Or is she committing it to memory?

"*Are you hungry?*" *he asked.* "*I can call the servant.*" *He himself felt he would never eat again.*

She shook her head and took a few steps forward. Lovely, he thought. This uncertainty in her eyes, so different from their usual coyness. Yesterday he would have found this intriguing, but yesterday he would not have flinched at her touch, and she would have looked at him as she used to, confident in her power to charm him. Now he can only compare them to another's eyes and the hurt he had seen there. "*I am not a whore.*" *The wine had done nothing to alleviate the shame of her words or chase away the memory of her eyes.*

"*I wore the dress,*" *the woman before him said finally, removing her shawl to reveal her marble-white shoulders and the rise of her breast just visible over the emerald-green brocade. It was a dress he had given her, and her dark eyes sought his approval.*

He had painted her before. She had dropped her dress around her, and he had placed her hand upon her breast as she looked at him with that alluring smile. "*She keeps you warm on cold nights?*" *Chigi had asked on seeing the painting for the first time. Raffaello had been evasive in his response, but it was this invitation to pleasure he had hoped to capture again. But could he, when he no longer desired her?*

"Take the chair by the window," Raffaello said. "And take down your hair." She seemed relieved and sat in the chair as he requested, pulling out the pins from her long dark hair. "Do not arrange it," he added. "Only let it fall as it pleases."

She did as she was told, regaining as she did so some of her usual confidence. "You will paint me against this background of old houses and laundry?"

He smiled, or came as close as he could to smiling this morning. "No, behind you will be hills and trees and—"

"And a castle?" she interrupted. He could see she hoped that all was well once again, that his aloofness was only temporary, the result of too much wine.

"If you would like a castle, I will paint you one," he said, feigning lightness. He took a long narrow strip of leather from among his brushes and bound back his hair before picking up the piece of charcoal he would use to begin his sketch.

She held one hand above her breast, the other cupped in her lap, palm up, and asked for his approval. He gave it, forcing into his voice the enthusiasm he did not feel.

This first stage of a painting usually moved quickly for him, the charcoal flying around the canvas, capturing his subject in a flurry of lines—a process that was more instinctive than calculated. Yet today seemed labored—for today he could not meet her eyes. His hand could not make her form. It was as if she were there in the room standing between them. Her head bent over a rose, her blue eyes soft as an early-morning sky, the gentle curve of her brow. The charcoal snapped in his hand, and he laid his free arm against the canvas and rested his forehead against it. He let the charcoal drop from his fingers, and it shattered on the floor.

"Are you ill?" she cried, leaping from her seat. She put her arm around him and attempted to steer him toward the bed. He raised his head from the canvas and carefully removed her arm.

"No. Please forgive me. I cannot paint this morning." He could barely hold her gaze.

She went slowly to the window and with her back to him began to replace the pins she had only just removed. "Shall I return later today?" she asked, but there was little hope in her voice.

I have offended her too, he thought as he apologized again. How could he explain to her that he had lost his enthusiasm for this painting, that he could not be sure it would ever return. There was only one woman he wanted to paint now. A woman, thanks to his own recklessness, he would never see again. He went to the window and, taking the remaining pins from her hands, finished fastening her hair.

He would speak to Chigi and arrange for her to be paid. He could do that much for her. She relied on this work he gave her, for she was only a baker's daughter. Theirs was a relationship based on a certain convenience, but that did not mean she did not care for him. Or he for her.

He rang the bell for his servant to see her home before taking the shawl from where she had left it and draping it over her shoulders. A simple gesture he had made so many times before. Was it for the last time? Could he see her again, knowing he longed for someone else.

She raised her face to him and he kissed her on the cheek, wondering as he did so if he would one day see her on the arm of another painter, her likeness in another's painting. Or would he glimpse her through a bakery door? Her alabaster skin reddened by the heat of the ovens, children clinging to floury apron strings?

He opened the door for her and went to the window as she stepped out into the street with his servant. She did not look up, but he raised his hand anyway and watched until she passed out of sight.

On an island of wild roses

The guidebook says this is one of the treasures of the lagoon islands. Sant'Erasmo—a round medieval fort, a field of artichokes, a stream with ducks. Crumbling, pastoral. But not anymore. The fort is still there, but bulldozers have ripped up the artichokes, leaving mounds of churned-up dirt, and the pastoral stream is now a muddy ditch that no self-respecting duck would call home. Tulia dutifully studies the plaque outlining the plans for the restoration. An artist's rendering shows lawns and gardens around a tidied-up fort. Admittedly it will be interesting, and it is good, isn't it, that its decay will be halted? Only she cannot help but think it is losing its poetry too.

Back on the gravel road, she removes one of her sandals and shakes out a stone. She takes a long drink of water from the bottle she carries in her bag, adjusts her straw hat, and hopes her sunscreen is as effective as promised. She plans to follow the road into the village and stop at a café before taking the vaporetto back to the main island. It is early afternoon, and the little lizards sunning themselves on the road scurry off into the grass, frightened by her shadow. Brilliant red poppies grow in fields toward neat rows of grapevines while along the road wild roses, fragrant in the heat of the day, cascade over fences and tangle in the hedges.

It has been two days since she saw Raphael, and she has purposely kept to these outer islands, reducing the chances she will run into him. But still, she can't avoid the city completely, and she has taken to scanning the faces of every gondolier she passes, half hoping, half fearing she will see him among them. She could have left Venice immediately of course, but she has fallen in love with the city and is determined not to let him ruin it for her.

"I wanted you to come to Italy," he told her, "so I bought the last ticket to Amsterdam. It seemed like the logical thing to do." Well, it wasn't logical, and she said so. He did not argue with her when she demanded he stop the gondola. Ignoring his proffered hand, she climbed out. "Don't even think of following me, Raphael—or whatever your name is," she said, turning around at the top of the steps, "or I'll call the police." Not that she would. What would she tell them? Surely they would say it was a coincidence. It is not impossible for travelers to cross paths more than once. She headed down the first street that led away from the canal, not caring where she was going, finally emerging on the south side of the island and catching a vaporetto back to her hotel. It wasn't until she closed the door of her room that she noticed she was still clutching the plane ticket.

Now she steps out of the road into the grass to let a couple of nuns on mopeds pass. In their long habits, black veils flapping behind them, the women make a strange sight. She watches until they disappear around the bend in a puff of dust, leaving in their wake the afternoon's heavy silence. She turns left onto the road that leads to the village and passes a walled cemetery, glimpsing garish flower arrangements through the open gate.

In her room she pushed the plane ticket between the pages of

Miss Mercy, not sure why she was keeping it. Evidence perhaps? But of what? At worst he was stalking her, at best he was manipulating her. Had she not seen him again after Paris, she would have been left with only good memories. But now her gullibility makes her feel rather ill.

Mostly, though, she feels lonely. So lonely that she came close to losing all her pride by calling Ethan. But she lost her nerve and hung up before his phone in New York even had a chance to ring. What would she have said to him? *Hi, I met this man, and even though he wouldn't tell me his real name, I think I was falling in love with him. But he turned out to be crazy, so are you really sure you want to leave me?*

Besides, what if Jasmine had been there? Perhaps she would even have answered the phone. She wouldn't have known what to say to her. It's not Jasmine's fault that she and Ethan are falling apart, but if Ethan has to have an affair, why can't it be with someone else?

Something else is worrying her too. Money. The hotel is far from cheap, and while Ethan said not to worry about the credit-card bills, she can't help but think that was before she learned about Jasmine. What if he decides not to pay and she finds herself over the limit? She has a little money of her own, but the hotel would eat it up in a matter of days, and all the inexpensive places are fully booked.

Almost worse than fretting about money is the feeling that she is being bought off, that Ethan is appeasing his guilt by funding her vacation. Perhaps she should move into the Gritti Palace Hotel and really make him pay. But she knows she won't, and she is sure Ethan knows it too. Besides, essentially she's been living off him for years. A few more weeks won't make a difference. He set the situation up this way so he could get together with Jasmine; she may as well let him continue to pay. So she settled her bill in advance at the front desk, holding her breath until her card was approved. She is paid up until Sunday. She will decide then what to do next.

There is a café across from the vaporetto stop, and except for a couple bent over a guidebook and glasses of beer, the tables outside are empty. Like the rest of the island, it is peaceful here, with no one else in sight. She can just make out the airport across the lagoon where every minute another plane takes off or lands, but it seems distant from this sleepy place.

She is deciding where to sit when the man looks up. *"Buongiorno,"* he says, clearly recognizing her. "You're staying at the Hotel Dolce Vita, aren't you?"

"Yes," she says, trying to place him among the other guests at the hotel.

"We saw you in the dining room last night, but I don't think you saw us. You looked so intent on your book." In reality she had been staring at her notebook and wondering if she had the heart to keep working on her novel when all she could really think about was how she'd been duped.

"I'm sorry," he continues. "We should introduce ourselves. I'm Matthew James, and this is my wife, Caroline. Care to join us?"

She accepts, their conversation coming as a welcome relief. She introduces herself. Matthew is a handsome man in his mid-thirties, tanned, successful-looking, with a kind smile and soft gray eyes. If Ethan and Raphael are on opposite ends of some sort of scale, then Matthew falls midway. Caroline seems to be the more reserved of the two, happy to let her husband do the talking, but she smiles when she shakes Tulia's hand. She too is very attractive, her lovely face shaded under a wide-brimmed hat. She seems so cool and unruffled, even in this heat. Her brilliant red lipstick is the same color as her sundress, and the overall impression is of a Hollywood actress from the forties. They make a striking couple, and Tulia can't help but think that everyone except herself is happy.

She vetoes Matthew's suggestion of beer or wine, saying either would put her to sleep instantly, and orders an espresso and a bottle of water *senza gas* instead.

"It's always nice to see a familiar face while traveling," he says. "It reminds me of when I was nineteen and backpacking around Europe. You'd meet someone in a hostel in Amsterdam and run into them again in the train station in Rome. Those were great times."

"Did that happen often?" she asks with interest.

"Well, only once," he confesses. "There was this woman I met on the flight from Toronto. We said good-bye in the airport in London, only to meet again in a nightclub in Paris. We decided it was too much of a coincidence to be anything other than fate and ended up traveling together." He turns to his wife. "And here we are."

Tulia feels momentary hope until she remembers that meeting Raphael was not a coincidence.

"You aren't being completely honest, Matthew," Caroline says a little reproachfully.

"What do you mean?" It's a question, but he is laughing. Tulia senses that this is a joke between them, and she has that all-too-familiar feeling of being an outsider.

"Don't listen to him," Caroline says. "He knew I was going to Paris. So he timed his arrival there to coincide with mine. But being from small-town Ontario, he underestimated just how big Paris was. He spent days scouring the streets for me. When he finally found me, I knew right away his surprise at seeing me was totally feigned."

"But you went along with it?"

"Of course. I thought it was sweet that he'd gone to so much trouble. He admitted everything after we were married and couldn't believe I'd already figured it out."

Matthew laughs again. "Okay, so it wasn't a complete coincidence. But it could have been." Tulia is wondering how their story differs from hers and Raphael's when Matthew asks her how long she's been in Venice.

"Almost a week," she says. "I leave on Sunday. And yourselves?"

"Only since yesterday, but we're here for two weeks. Where are you off to next?"

"I don't know," she says honestly. In a moment of optimism about her new book, she canceled both her bus tour and the bed-and-breakfast in England. "I think I'll see more of Italy. Rome or Florence perhaps." She doesn't know right now if she'll continue working on the novel, but at least she can see the places of importance to Raffaello and hope this rekindles her enthusiasm.

"Either choice is a good one," Matthew says, "although the noise and traffic is sufficient to ruin both places for us. We're sticking to Venice this trip. It's so much quieter—one can walk in the streets without fear of being run down. Even on this island, where scooters and bicycles are allowed, they don't take over. I love sitting in a café like this and looking out over the lagoon or a canal."

"It is special," she agrees, already nostalgic for it.

"And you have found Sant'Erasmo. Not many tourists come this far from the city."

"I came to see the fort," she says, half turning to engage Caroline in the conversation, but she is gazing out over the lagoon, seemingly lost in thought.

"Ah." Matthew's face clouds. "I almost forgot how upset I was by the sight of the fort. You would not believe how pretty it once was."

"I can imagine," she replies. "I've been trying to decide whether restoring it is a good thing. I mean, it's important that it not just disappear."

"You're perhaps right, but I fear it's being restored for the benefit of the tourist trade rather than out of any real concern for history. There was no need to destroy the stream or plow under the artichokes. I worry that someday Venice will no longer be a city where people live but just a giant tourist theme park surrounded by ugly suburbs. Sometimes I think it would be better if Venice did just slip away under the sea and be spared such a horrible fate."

"I hope neither comes true. I think Venice is pretty resilient. The tourists, the cruise ships, even those planes taking off and landing every minute can't take away from the magic. And we have to remember that we're tourists too."

"Touché. You're absolutely right." His laugh is clear and natural. Why couldn't she meet someone like him? She thinks Caroline is pretty lucky.

As if on cue, Caroline turns to Tulia and smiles encouragingly. "We're on our way to Burano. Have you been there yet?"

"Just yesterday. You'll like it—it's so colorful. Every garden overflows with roses, and the houses are the most wonderful colors, pink and blue and mauve. Somehow even the laundry drying on the clotheslines manages to look postcard perfect."

"That's a wonderful recommendation. We'll look forward to it. And what do you do, Tulia, when not in Venice?"

It is the question she has come to hate, and she is suddenly less comfortable. "I work in a bookstore in New York. I'm also a writer of sorts." She sips her water. It is already warm.

"Of sorts? What does that mean?"

Why does she insist on telling the truth? Why doesn't she just end it with the bookstore? "Well, I published a novel a couple of years ago," she explains, "but since then I've had writer's block. I started something new on this trip, but I'm afraid it isn't going very well."

"What's the name of the book that was published?" Caroline asks.

"It's called *Heaven on Earth*."

Caroline ponders for a moment. "No, I'm afraid I haven't heard of it." She looks at her husband, but he shakes his head apologetically.

"We'll certainly look forward to reading it," he says with enthusiasm.

"I doubt you'd like it. It's just a romance really."

"Don't be so hard on yourself," he says. "A bit of romance never hurt anyone. What's your new book about?"

"I've only just started my research, but I think it's going to be a fictitious account of the painter Raphael's life." She uses the English form of the name, the image of the sidewalk artist flashing before her. Has she overreacted? Matthew followed Caroline to Paris, and Caroline thought it was romantic. Raphael followed her to Venice, and she concluded she was being stalked.

"Raphael," says Caroline. "That sounds interesting. But I'm afraid you really will have to brave Rome and Florence, for those were truly Raphael's cities. There is nothing by Raphael in Venice."

"There's Titian's *Assumption of the Virgin* in the Frari," Matthew suggests. "You can see the influence on Raphael's last work, *The Transfiguration*. But no one knows whether Raphael traveled to Venice to see it or whether the painting traveled to Rome."

"And while you're at the Frari," Caroline adds, "you can see the baby Jesus that Matthew and I have decided must be the most hideous rendition of an infant, divine or otherwise, ever."

"It's our ongoing quest," he explains. "Some truly terrible depictions of the Madonna and child have been churned out over the centuries. Perhaps it's a bit cruel of us, but we take delight in trying to find the worst."

"You both seem to know a lot about Renaissance art," Tulia says.

"Caroline is the art history professor," he says. "My area is Native American studies."

"You know, there's also a romance in Raphael's story," Caroline says. "The baker's daughter, his model for the painting *La Fornarina*."

"I know," Tulia says. "But I want to give him a new lover. Not the baker's daughter. It bothers me because my imagination is taking me in a different direction from the facts."

A small crowd collects on the dock, signaling the arrival of the vaporetto, and Matthew and Caroline gather their things. "I know you've already been, but would you like to come to Burano with us?" Matthew asks. "We could have a late lunch together. You can tell us more about your book and this new lover of Raphael's."

Tulia declines. She is tired, and the thought of discussing Raphael's new lover depresses her. Which Raphael? What new lover? It certainly isn't her.

A new story begins

When Tulia was born, her mother was almost fifty. A menopause baby, Tulia has since heard this phenomenon called. Her parents never made a conscious decision not to have children, but as involved as they were in their careers, they could never foresee having time for a child.

And she is certain even now they never got over the surprise of her arrival. Whenever she came into the room, they always looked up with a bewildered expression on their faces as if wondering how this strange child came to be in their house. She always had the feeling that she never quite belonged in the world her parents had made for themselves. They were out of place too among the youthful parents of her friends, some of whom had been their students.

Her father especially never quite knew what to do with her as a child. Perhaps fittingly for a professor of Restoration literature, he didn't even have a concept of what a child was beyond being a very small adult. It was the Victorians who decided children were distinct from adults, requiring play and a certain shielding from the realities of the adult world.

He scoffed at the children's books that were given to her as presents, instead reading to her from the *Norton Anthology of English Literature,* starting with Chaucer. And as other children might have heard *The Cat in the Hat* so many times they knew it by heart, so Tulia knew the poetry of Alexander Pope, her father's specialty.

> In woods bright Venus with Adonis stray'd
> And chaste Diana haunts the forest shade.

Not what most people would consider appropriate for a child.

On occasion she sat in on his lectures and knew he was prone to forget where he was, quoting long passages of Pope, a faraway look in his eye that she is now sure was mimicked by many an undergraduate student over drinks at the campus pub.

From learning Pope to writing *Heaven on Earth.* Her parents had congratulated her achievement, and if they were disappointed her writing hadn't taken a more literary bent, they hadn't let on. Maybe *Heaven on Earth* was her answer to adolescent rebellion, or, thinking again of Pope's heavily suggestive lines, perhaps it wasn't such a stretch after all. She would never tell her father this though.

While her mother wasn't quite as scornful of children's books as her father, nevertheless Tulia also grew up on *Beowulf,* her mother's forté. She learned to read Old English almost before the "See Spot run" of her first-grade reader. Her mother had most encouraged her writing, and Tulia filled the notebooks she bought her, often with serials hundreds of pages long. One particular epic about a young heiress kidnapped by evil teachers kept her occupied through most of her eleventh year. Her story had a happy ending, with the evil teachers penitent for their transgressions and the girl reunited with her real mother and father, who showered her with attention. Tulia now knows wishful thinking certainly played a large role in the plot, not unlike *Heaven on Earth.*

She had friends but they rarely came to the house. There the atmosphere had the hushed quality of a library, and loud play seemed somehow disrespectful. Only at the cabin in the Poconos did the hush feel less oppressive. Perhaps that explained her attachment to the place.

She sometimes wonders how her parents really felt after she left home, imagining them settling with a sigh back into their just-the-two-of-them existence, quiet flowing over and filling her empty place.

She shares some of this with Matthew over a glass of wine. While she turned down the offer to visit Burano earlier that day, she did go with Matthew and Caroline to hear Vivaldi's *Four Seasons* at the Scuola di San Rocco. Upon their return to the hotel, Caroline, pleading tiredness, went to bed. Tulia, not wanting the music to leave her, was happy to accept Matthew's invitation to continue the evening.

He too had an unconventional childhood. His parents divorced when he was three, and his time was divided between his mother, a classics professor in a small university town, and his playwright father and elderly grandmother who lived on the reserve nearby. "Half Italian-Canadian, half Mohawk," he says. "It was a never-ending cycle of culture shock." Maybe, Tulia thinks, the "conventional" childhood she always dreamed of only exists in her imagination. Still, hers really was a lonely childhood, if not a terrible one.

After they part around midnight, Tulia changes into her white cotton nightgown and opens the windows to her balcony, where lightning flashes across the indigo sky. Two cats huddle in the murky shadows of the doorway in the palazzo across the canal, their eyes blinking yellow. She's amazed by the number of cats in Venice. On her first day she tried to pet one and only narrowly escaped being bitten. Since then, she has admired them from a safe distance.

She leaves her balcony door open and lying in bed listens to the lonesome patter of rain on the canal, the deep rumblings of thunder that remind her of summers spent in the mountains. She will look for Raphael tomorrow. Perhaps it was the music that filled her with such conviction. Or maybe it was being with Matthew and Caroline and knowing the history of their meeting. Whatever the reason, she knows if she doesn't try to find him again, she will regret it, always looking back and wondering what might have been.

She means to proceed with caution. For even if she is willing to accept the way he manipulated their meeting in Venice, there is still the question of his name. She should have asked Caroline what she would have done if Matthew had been evasive about his name—would she still have thought him "sweet"? But as she didn't ask, she resolves to make it a condition of forgiving Raphael when—and if—she finds him.

After a blissfully dreamless sleep, she awakes to the roar of a water taxi traveling at some illegal speed past her window. She showers, dresses in a sleeveless turquoise cotton sundress, and starts her search. But, confident or not that she is doing the right thing, how can she actually hope to find him? The city is small, but that does not mean they will cross paths, and that also assumes he is still here. And while she still thinks of him as a French sidewalk artist, it appears she is wrong and he is really an Italian gondolier. She could ask another gondolier, but again she doesn't know his name, and to describe him—dark eyes, long dark hair—could describe a lot of men.

At San Marco, she does not see him among the gondoliers gathered there or working on the surrounding canals. After wandering for an hour, she finds herself in Campo Santa Margherita, where she orders a cappuccino and pastry for a late breakfast. A sparrow lands boldly on the table in front of her, stealing crumbs from the edge of her plate. Remembering that Raphael fed crumbs to a sparrow on the day she shared his lunch on the bank of the Seine, she takes this as a good sign.

The morning air is fresh and cool after the night of rain, but already the sun has dried the last of the puddles in Santa Margherita. She pays her bill and walks out among the morning shoppers laden with fruits and vegetables from the stalls in the *campo*. Is there a place where she could leave a message for him? A union hall or a bar where gondoliers hang out? But what would she say in such a message, and would he get it before she leaves Venice the next day? She is still unsure where she will go next.

Planting her sunglasses on top of her head, she goes through a rack of postcards at a news kiosk. She phoned her parents when she first reached Venice but has yet to send them anything. She settles on a black-and-white reproduction of a vintage postcard of the *campo*, thinking that except for the clothing styles, it didn't look much different from today.

She is putting it in her purse when the oranges catch her eye. They are blood oranges from Sicily, their thick skins more red than orange. Some are wrapped in bright red paper decorated with dragons. Neatly packed in crates, they are stacked up beside a market table. *"Due, per favore,"* she says and, not knowing the Italian word for oranges, points them out to the stall's proprietor.

"Arancia. That is the word for orange. It is a good word." The voice comes from behind her, and she whirls around. "Are you sure you only want two? I will buy them all for you."

He wears his familiar vest, the birds and flowers catching the sun. He doesn't look like a gondolier today. She mumbles something about two being enough. Finishing the transaction, he hands her the brown paper bag.

"How did you find me?" she says after thanking him. It is too crazy that she was looking for him only for him to find her.

"It is a small town, *cara,*" he says, as if that explains everything. He takes her arm, and they step away from the stall, passing through the shade of a tree. "Are you still angry at me?" He smiles at her as if he already knows her answer.

And she isn't. She is only relieved. But she has put conditions on forgiving him. "I think you have a lot of explaining to do."

"What would you like me to explain?"

"Why did you have that ticket from Paris to Amsterdam?"

"Because I wanted you to come to Italy," he says, repeating what he told her days earlier in the gondola. "So I bought the last ticket to Amsterdam. I do not understand why you think that is not logical."

"For a million reasons. Like, why wouldn't I just take the next flight to Amsterdam? And how did you know that I would come to Venice instead?"

They turn out of the *campo* and walk along the *calla* past the gelato stand, the supermarket, and the mask maker's shop before stopping on a bridge. Moored alongside is a barge selling yet more fruits and vegetables. "Because the next flight to Amsterdam was also sold out," he says. "And I knew you were interested in the painter Raffaello. If you could not go to Holland, I knew you would get the idea to come to Italy. And Venezia was the next available flight. See, is that not logical, *cara?*"

It is logical in some crazy way, and he seems so earnest, so concerned she understand him, that she laughs.

"What?" he says. "What now?"

She takes a deep breath and tries to speak but is overwhelmed by the laughter. She leans back against the parapet of the bridge and squints up at the dazzling noon sun. It feels so good to laugh—so hard the tears run down her cheeks. The anger over Ethan and Jasmine floats away over the roofs of the palazzi. So does her fear of that dream. Her loneliness. Her money problems. Her book. All of it. She is in Venice with Raphael, and everything, absolutely everything, is possible.

Suddenly his face is between her and the sky, haloed by the sun, and she finally stops laughing. Hilarity dissolving into desire.

"I am so relieved," he says. He seems oblivious to her new state, brushing aside her tears as if she were a child, using a handkerchief from his pocket. "I thought for a moment you might have gone mad."

Desire forgotten, she laughs again, as much at his choice of the old-fashioned term as at the insinuation itself. "Me, mad?! It's you who's mad!"

"Me?" That guileless look again.

"Yes, you! Why didn't you just ask me to come to Italy? Instead you let me believe that I'd never see you again. And then that plane ticket. What was I supposed to think? You scared me, Raphael."

He looks confused. "I am sorry," he says finally. "I did not mean to frighten you. I only wanted to give you time to work things through with Ethan. I thought this would be a good surprise." He looks down at the water, still seemingly puzzled that his behavior should be construed as odd.

She feels only tenderness now. How could she have thought he was dangerous? How is this really different from pulling flowers from his sleeve or releasing balloons from the Eiffel Tower?

"Do you mean, then," he says very slowly, "that I just should have told you I wanted to meet you in Venezia?"

"Of course," she says with quiet certainty. "Not everything has to be a magic trick, you know."

He nods as if he finally understands. Then he takes her arm, and they turn back in the direction of the Frari. "So you will meet me in Firenze?"

It is not until that night back in her hotel room that she remembers she wasn't going to forgive him until he told her his real name. She forgot—but she has also forgotten what there was to forgive.

Hoping to reach you

*M*y Beloved—

How I long to know your name! I write to you from Firenze, and send this letter through a trusted servant. To stay in Roma was unbearable knowing you were there, so close, and yet I could not see you.

If only I could take back the moment I caused you offense! If only I could make you understand how much I have suffered for it since! I caused you shame, and for that I die a little every day. I only pray that God in His infinite mercy will give me the words that will lead to my redemption in your eyes. I pray that you read these words with an open heart and believe that I write them with God as my witness.

I should never have been so disrespectful as to read your work without your permission. I can only say in my defense that, once I started to read, I was powerless to stop. What a gift you possess—do not hide it from the world! If I can help, I beg you, let me. If you only let me into your life for this one purpose, that I might ease your situation so that you may devote yourself to your writings, I will be content. My wealth then will have been put to a most noble purpose.

But having written the above, I know I could never be happy with just that. It is not only with the desire to be your patron that I write. I did not ever plan to buy your affections. Only—I desired and still do with every beat of my heart—that you should feel even for a moment what I have felt for you since I saw you in the market buying oranges.

Please, I beg of you, do not let this letter go unanswered. I long to see you again. I cannot sleep. I cannot work. And all beauty in the world pales against the memory of you. May God be with you and protect you and find a way in His wisdom to open your heart to my pleas.

I remain yours forever—
Raffaello Sanzio
Firenze, May 1519

Raffaello Sanzio—

Do I dare believe you? I found your letter on my doorstep and pressed it close to my heart, thinking how you had held it only days before with your own hands.

That afternoon, I sat with you in the garden and felt at least for you what you say you felt for me, only to think later that it was all flattery and bribery. Raffaello Sanzio has loved many women. You have not gone unnoticed in Roma.

You asked me how it is that I live here. It is not so long a story as I said. I am the only legitimate child of a Venetian merchant. My mother died while giving birth to me, and my father never forgave me for it. He dutifully raised a good dowry for me and desired that I should wed the son of a local nobleman. But when I met my future husband at the betrothal, I knew I could not marry him. I could not be condemned to live the rest of my life with a man of no spirit, with no love for beauty, for art, for nature. He is a man who lives for the hunt and war. For death. I knew if I married him that I would die inside too. And while tradition says I have a right to refuse, my father did not accept my decision graciously. Hence my banishment. I stay here in this little house thanks to my mother's brother who took pity on me.

But his generosity has limits. He has daughters who need dowries of their own, and thus my state is a precarious one. Until now I have made a meager existence translating texts for a friend of my uncle's. But my source of texts is by last reports dying and no longer in need of my services. I am very sensitive to the truth that many women like me have found sustenance only by becoming courtesans. I would sooner die. And it is in this context that our meeting took place.

So now, having thrown you from my house, I find myself looking to you for deliverance of both my body and soul. Raffaello Sanzio, painter of angels, while I think that your desire may have made you overly generous in your appraisal of my talents, I accept your offer of a patronage. Your tremendous influence may even overcome the disadvantage of my sex.

But more, I will entrust my heart to you. It has not been given to anyone before, and I do not give it to you lightly. As a sign of your love for me, I ask that you keep our relationship a secret. I will not be known as anyone's mistress. Not even of the great Raffaello Sanzio.

Send your servant, and I will join you in Firenze.

I dream of our meeting—
Your Beloved
Roma, May 1519

To: Tulia
From: Ethan
Subject: Re: Re: **I almost forgot**

Tulia:

Am about to run to a meeting now with our biggest client.
Glad to hear you've met someone traveling—have fun. Had a
blast at the game with Jasmine—the Yankees won!

Ethan ☻

Reply

Dear Ethan:

Delete

Where it all began

Urbino, unlike Venice, is not crawling with tourists. Sandwiched between Tuscany and the Adriatic Sea in a region of the Apennine foothills known as the Marches, it is not on the main sightseeing circuit. It took Tulia the better part of a day to travel here, including several train and bus transfers, all the while lugging her baggage with its increasingly heavy collection of books and notes on Raffaello.

She has gotten an early start in the cool of the morning, a brief blessing really, because it's clear the day will be sweltering. She walks up the steep and narrow cobblestone streets lined with plain medieval and more elaborate Renaissance-era houses. The byways bustle with people, mostly students on their way to class at the university. She is heading to the Ducal Palace, built, so the small entry in her guidebook tells her, during Urbino's time of greatest splendor in the fifteenth century under the reign of the illustrious Duke Federico of Montefeltro.

She admires the building's graceful architecture as it comes into view. The setting for the courtly life chronicled in Castiglione's

The Courtier, the palace is enchanting, constructed by the duke on the ruins of an ancient fortress. As an enlightened humanist and patron of the arts, the duke and his benevolent rule fashioned Urbino into one of the most civilized cities in Renaissance Italy. And into this environment one of Italy's most famous sons was born—Raffaello Sanzio.

The palace is now a museum containing paintings by Urbino artists. Once inside, Tulia quickly skims through the sparsely decorated rooms with names like the Chapel of Forgiveness and the Temple of the Muses until she finds the only painting there done by Raffaello. *La Muta,* The Silent Woman. Tulia wonders if the unknown model was another of Raffaello's lovers, one who preceded the baker's daughter.

She arrives at the Casa Natale di Raffaello, Raffaello's birthplace, just as the doors swing open. This is the reason she has come to Urbino—to see where Raffaello grew up, to understand how his formative years in Urbino shaped his adulthood in Florence and Rome.

Besides, it is much better being here than spending four days waiting in Florence. For while Raphael asked her to meet him there, he wasn't willing to abandon his mysterious ways completely. When she asked exactly when and where in Florence they would meet, he only laughed and said, *Not to worry, cara. I will see you on Wednesday. You just enjoy yourself. I have business to which I must attend, but I will find you. I always do.*

Whitewashed walls gleaming in the sunlight, Raffaello's childhood home is grand by Renaissance standards, with several large rooms making up the living quarters. Raffaello's father, Giovanni, who was a painter in Federico's court, apparently made a good living from his craft at a time when painters were gaining increased respect.

She stops in front of a Madonna and Christ child painted on

one of the walls. It is not known for sure whether Raffaello or his father created this delicate scene between mother and baby. Her guidebook notes that scholars generally suspect the hand of Giovanni, with the model for the Madonna his wife and the study for the Christ child Raffaello himself. In fact, she learns, if one looks hard enough, Raffaello's boyhood likeness can be found in paintings and frescoes throughout Urbino, his thick brown hair falling to his shoulders, his angelic face looking up in wonder at the world around him.

After exiting the private apartments, she enters the courtyard and crosses to the studio where Giovanni kept his apprentices busy with commissions and his son occupied with education. Here is where Raffaello himself likely first picked up a brush, ordained to be a painter from birth because of his father's profession. At first he probably imitated his father as the elder Sanzio demonstrated his own techniques and tricks of the trade. She sees the stone where the pair ground their colors and imagines them working side by side. Although Giovanni died when Raffaello was only eleven, he had already recognized that his son, with his extraordinary talent, would far surpass his own achievements.

Outside the house, as she rests in the shade of a nearby wall, she stares down at the cobblestones. Had Raffaello himself run over them on his way to buy bread for his mother or pigments for his father? Scuffed them with his shoes as he walked with Giovanni to an appointment at the Ducal Palace?

The sun beats down hot and heavy, and sweat runs down her brow as she makes her way up a hill. Her hair is pulled back into a ponytail, and her white blouse sticks to her shoulders and back. As she shifts her day pack from one arm to the other, she wishes she had remembered to wear her straw hat.

Finally she reaches the greenery and flowers of Fortezza Albornoz at the top of the hill, grateful for the trees that afford plenty of shade. She wanders around the old fort and the gardens before settling on an empty bench, where she unwraps her *panino* and bottled water. From this vantage point, she can see a church in the distance (Federico's burial place, the guidebook tells her), undulating green hills, the high stone walls that mark the city limits, and the fanciful Ducal Palace, all settings for Raffaello's paintings.

Two little boys, maybe six or seven years old, skip through the gardens holding hands. They are laughing until one of them trips and starts to cry, rolling in the grass and clutching his leg. Not seeing a mother or other caregiver, Tulia runs over to him and, speaking soothingly, looks at his leg, relieved to see it is only a scraped knee. The boys are talking over each other at her in Italian, totally ignoring her apologetic *Non parlo italiano*. She takes her bottle and pours some water on the dirty, skinned knee, then blots the scrape with a tissue she finds in her pocket. They are handsome children, with dark intelligent eyes and, now that the crisis is over, ready smiles. If she was to have a child with Raphael, would he or she look like these children? Don't get ahead of yourself, she tells herself as the boys run off again calling *Grazie, grazie, grazie* over their shoulder.

Did Raffaello ever play in these gardens? She imagines him getting into mischief with some close friend. She knows his childhood was short-lived, not an atypical phenomenon during Renaissance times. Both parents had died by the time he was eleven. It must have been very lonely for Raffaello. An orphan at such a young age, and no mention of any siblings. On his own in the world. Exactly the way she often felt growing up as an only child. Sometimes she imagined she was an orphan, sent to live with distant relatives who cared for her due to familial obligation, provided for but never truly loved or wanted. As when her parents sent her to boarding school in Indiana the year after their sabbatical in England. She cried for days before they finally picked her up, admitting that perhaps it wasn't such a good idea after all.

As for the sidewalk artist, she knows nothing about his childhood. In fact, he has never mentioned family at all. Does he have a brother or sister? Does he get along with his mother and father? Do they encourage his talent? What do they think of his wandering artistic endeavors? Do they wish he had a "real" job? Or maybe his family is dead, killed in some tragic accident. Maybe he has an inheritance or trust fund, which would explain the fact that he never seems to care about money and can give it all away to a homeless man without thinking twice.

She finishes her sandwich. It is still stiflingly hot, so she decides to take advantage of the shade a little longer. She yawns and looks around. She would like to go back to her hotel for a nap, but it is so far away and the garden is so peaceful. Using her lumpy day pack as a pillow, she stretches out on the bench and closes her eyes, listening to the distant hum of traffic. A nearby church bell chimes once, and the slightest hint of a breeze brushes her skin as she starts to doze.

Suddenly, she jerks awake, nearly falling off the bench. She breathes heavily and is sweating again, though this time not from the sun. It's that dream again. The abyss. The total desolation. A figure emerging from the fog. It is the woman at her desk, that comb in her hair.

She tries to block out the images, but then Raphael's words come back to her. *All I know,* cara, *is that dreams often have something to tell us. But please do not be frightened.*

So she forces herself to go back through the details. The woman. Paper before her. An ink bottle. Holding a pen, maybe a quill. Not writing but looking out a window. Rain. Wiping the tears from her cheeks with her free hand. Smoothing her dark hair, her fingers lingering over each raised stone of the comb.

Tulia feels like crying herself. She is no longer frightened, just impossibly sad for this woman who is so clearly distraught. Why is she crying? She is sure now that this woman is the woman with the oranges, Raffaello's true love.

The gardens are as still as a cemetery, though she can sense a break in the oppressive humidity. She reaches into a side pocket of her bag and pulls out *On the Trail of the Writer,* but Urbino is too far off the beaten track for even the adventurous Miss Mercy. So instead, she takes out the *International Herald Tribune* she bought at a newsstand this morning. She skims the cover articles—bad news as usual, the kind that make her own problems seem so small. On the second page is an article on the latest scheme to save Venice from the sea, followed by a confirmation that Italy is in the grips of a heat wave, but it's the next headline that really grabs her attention.

Disappearance of Art Student
Raises Suspicions Across Europe

PARIS—The detective leading the investigation into the disappearance of an English art student in Paris says the probe could be widened to include "a handful of cases" from other European cities.

"The connection to the other cases is still tenuous but worth considering," said Detective Amir Ali. "What caught my eye was a report from the police in Milan concerning an American tourist abducted by a man who matches the description of the suspect being sought in the disappearance in Paris. While the American woman escaped unharmed, she was robbed of her passport, credit cards, and money. She said the man threatened her with physical harm if she did not cooperate."

Meanwhile, the search continues for the missing art student, who is now feared dead. The day before her disappearance, the student, whose name still has not been released, told a classmate at the Sorbonne that she had met an artist whom she had invited to her upcoming art show. She had described the man as very attractive, about 1.8 meters (6 feet) with shoulder-length dark hair and brown eyes who spoke excellent English with a "charming accent."

The art student had hinted at a possible meeting with the man the same evening of her disappearance. "She clearly was smitten with him," classmate Yukiko Otsuka reported. The missing woman is described as twenty-five years old, 1.6 meters (5 feet, 6 inches) with long blond hair and hazel eyes. On the day of her disappearance she was wearing a short black skirt and a sleeveless, light blue sweater.

Meanwhile, Detective Ali cautions female tourists to use common sense when traveling through Western Europe and to report any suspicions to the nearest police station.

Oh my God, could it be? Could it really be Raphael? Dark hair and eyes, speaks with an accent, claims to be an artist. Appears to be following her. But always disappearing. Is preying on other unsuspecting women the "business" he's always attending to? And now a possible murder? The missing woman sounds just like that English art student who invited Raphael to her opening. He pocketed that invitation. Did he go to the gallery? Could it be the same student?

Tulia can't believe it. Why did she have to go and find him again? This man could be a con artist, a swindler, a stalker, worse yet, a possible murderer. He has been following her since they met in Paris. True, she still has her passport and credit card, and no money has gone missing. But clearly he has been getting his money from other sources. Inheritance indeed. So maybe he has something worse in store for her. His next target in some drawn-out twisted game. Why has she been so naïve?

She has to find the nearest police station. She has to tell them what she knows, that she saw this guy two days ago in Venice. Presumably just before he went to Milan and robbed that poor girl. She feels enraged. And stupid too. To think she trusted him, told him so many things about herself, about her writing, about Ethan. She can't even admit that maybe she was falling in love with him or only moments ago was wondering what their children would look like.

With map in hand, she rushes to the nearest carabinieri station and plunges through the door. But once inside, she hesitates. What exactly will she tell the police? Will they think she's crazy? Do they even understand English? It's not as if she has an actual crime to report, just knowledge of an artist who matches the suspect's description.

No, more than that. She saw the missing woman too. It can't be just a coincidence. She won't be able to forgive herself if someone gets hurt because she doesn't report her suspicions. Besides, if he *is* guilty and she doesn't report him, isn't that aiding and abetting or something? And if he's not guilty, then surely he can clear himself by proving he was elsewhere.

"*Sì?*" A tall, young police officer stands behind a counter, looking like he's just woken up. Holding a cup of espresso, he can barely tear his eyes away from the muted TV suspended from the ceiling to look at Tulia standing in the doorway.

"*Scusi,*" she says, digging into her day pack for her Italian phrase book and the article. Downing his espresso, the officer looks back at the screen. A typical Italian show is on, with provocatively dressed singers and dancers and a lively male host. "*Problema,*" she says, pointing to the article. "*Uomo.* This man." Then she points to herself.

Finally looking directly at her, the officer starts speaking in Italian. A question, she tells herself. He's asking a question.

"I think I know who this man is—someone I saw in Venice. *Venezia,*" she adds, more loudly than necessary, as if a higher volume is all that is needed to be understood. Just like a typical tourist, she thinks.

"*No, no, no. È Urbino,*" says the officer as he taps the countertop.

She shakes her head vigorously. He must consider her an idiot not even to know what town she's in. "Venezia. I may know this *uomo.* I saw him in Venezia. And Paris. I may have even met this woman." She points again at the article, then realizes that he probably won't read English any better than he speaks it. She forges on, hoping that something will make sense. "I'm going to be meeting him in Florence. I mean Firenze." Again she speaks too loudly.

He shrugs offhandedly and calls back to the office behind him. Another officer eventually emerges, this one older and stouter with an enormous mustache. He looks annoyed to be summoned. "*Sì?*" he says brusquely.

"*Parla inglese?*" she asks, feeling helpless.

"A little," he says, his irritated expression not changing.

"I think I know who this man is," she says, showing him the article. Apparently dismissed from the conversation, the other officer goes back to watching TV.

Mustache is unimpressed. "He is boyfriend?"

"No. Yes. I don't know. But he could be this man here," she says, shaking the newspaper. "I met him in Paris, and we traveled together in Venice. I mean Venezia. We're going to meet in Firenze in a few days. You can find him there." Mustache glances up at the flashing TV screen, and she wonders if he can't read the English or simply can't be bothered to help. Maybe she should show him the plane ticket she now carries in her Miss Mercy book. But how to explain it?

He turns back to her. "You had fight?"

"I guess you could say that. In Venice." She is confused. Is this really relevant?

"Lover's fight," he says. "You are very pretty woman. No problem to find a different man. *Buona fortuna.*" And he dismisses her with a wave of his hand.

"No, no," she says, desperately wishing she knew some Italian. "I think he's the artist. The one from Paris."

Mustache shakes his head. "Sorry. No help." He turns away.

"Wait!" Does he think she's making this up because of some lover's quarrel? "He could be dangerous." She speaks very slowly and deliberately, more and more convinced she is doing the right thing. "The police in Florence should question him."

Mustache abruptly barks an order to his colleague, who starts to rummage behind the counter. He emerges with a one-inch stack of forms that he pushes toward her.

"You want to find your boyfriend," Mustache says. "Fill these out, signorina. *Grazie, ciao.*" He lumbers over to an elaborate espresso maker.

She swears under her breath as she takes a look at the forms. All in Italian. She has no idea how to fill them out. And it would probably be useless anyway, since nobody around here is interested in what she has to say and they are only giving her these papers to get rid of her. Plus they seem to be a missing person's report, which is all wrong anyway.

She flips through the stack, trying to decipher the words, still not quite fathoming how wrong she seems to have been about Raphael. To think he was luring her to Florence. She's escaped from his clutches twice—no, three times. That sounds so melodramatic—escaping from his clutches—but what if she's not so lucky again? She will have to go to the police in Florence. They'll speak English there. She'll show them the plane ticket. Perhaps she should even call the American Embassy in Rome.

As she makes her plan, the door swings open, and a petite blond woman with an enormous pack on her back walks in. *"Ho trovato questo passaporto nella strada,"* she says confidently, giving the passport she has found to Mustache.

Tulia can't believe it when the old curmudgeon gives this woman an enormous smile and hands her an espresso. The younger officer takes out another form and starts filling it out himself. They can't seem to help her enough.

"Do you speak English?" Tulia asks desperately.

"Yes," she says. "Can I help you?"

"I'm wondering if you can translate for me."

"I can try." Tulia thinks her accent is Australian.

Tulia shows her the newspaper article. "I'm trying to explain to these officers that I may know the man they're looking for. But I don't think they understand," Tulia says, showing her the newspaper article. "They've given me a missing person's form to fill out instead."

The woman says something in Italian to the officers. Mustache replies before going into one of the back offices.

"He says the Spanish police just captured the bloke this morning in Madrid," the woman explains. "They have a fax they can show you."

They've caught him! She's safe. He's behind bars and won't be able to harm anyone else. She feels relief, but at the same time a rush of disappointment. So it really is over. No more surprises, no more adventure. Should she even bother going to Florence? She will never finish her book now. Every time she tries to write about Raffaello the painter, she will envision this stalker.

Mustache emerges with a sheet of paper and places it on the

counter. Tulia forces herself to look, wanting to get this over with as quickly as possible. At least now she will have the peace of mind that he is no longer following her.

"He's being held without bail," the Australian woman translates.

But it's not Raphael! The man in the photo is heavier than the sidewalk artist, with a more pronounced nose, and his eyes look mean. Eyes so completely unlike Raphael's warm, comforting ones.

"You know this guy?" the Australian woman asks with interest.

"I thought I did," Tulia says, feeling a little embarrassed but mostly joyful. "Thank God I was wrong. I don't know what I would've done if you weren't here to translate for me." She hands the stack of forms back to the young officer. *"Grazie,"* she says to everyone, but they appear to have already forgotten about her. Mustache is making more espresso before she is even out the door.

She is so relieved, ecstatic even. There is no reason to think he wants to cause her harm. In fact, the opposite. She's simply going to have to trust him and accept the fact that he'll tell her things when he's ready. Like his real name. Though now she can't imagine calling him anything but Raphael.

And begins again

Ever since he had dispatched the servant with his letter, he had lived in a state of constant dread—not believing his pleas would be answered, not knowing how he would go on living if they were not. Even here in Firenze, the city of his youth, he had been unable to find solace, leaving his apartments only to visit this tiny church and light candles for a favorable reply. But not only had she answered, she had signed the letter "Your Beloved."

"Hail Mary, full of grace . . ." He could scarcely concentrate on the words. He had prayed so hard and now gave thanks, but the words of her letter kept intruding on his prayers to the Virgin. "Hail Mary, full of grace . . . I dream of our meeting . . . the Lord is with thee . . . Your Beloved . . . Your Beloved . . ."

He left the church having lit every candle and made his way up the steep cobbled streets. It was midday, and the shops were shuttered and quiet. He had no destination in mind, but he could not return to his apartments for they were too small and dark to contain so much joy.

He left behind the shops and continued in the direction of the Basilica San Miniato al Monte. At the top of the hill he looked down on the city blanketed with red-tiled roofs. Firenze was best viewed from above, beyond the stench of the Arno River and the butcher shops that lined the Ponte Vecchio. Above the roofs rose the Duomo, Giotto's Belltower, the campanile of the Palazzo Vecchio in the Piazza della Signoria, the Baptistry, the Church of Santa Croce. And beyond the man-made splendors, the golden hills of the Tuscan countryside.

It was a view he loved, and yet he scarcely saw it, having once again drawn her letter from inside his cloak. He left the road, walked down the grassy slope, and stretched out between the trees. He read it again and again, savoring the shape of every letter, word, phrase, seeing in them the wonderful promise of a future together.

While awaiting her reply, he had convinced himself he would, despite the wording of his own letter, be content with simply being her patron. But she had answered all his prayers. "I will entrust my heart to you." And if he could not tell anyone of their love, it was a small price to pay.

He would of course send servants on the morrow to meet her and bring her here. But should he also send for an apprentice, for his paints and brushes and work here in Firenze? Take on some commissions or start something new? God knew how much he wished to paint his . . . here he paused in his thoughts as if to prepare himself for the immense significance of the words . . . his beloved. His students in Roma could look after his work in his absence. He would leave Giulio Romano, his most talented student, in charge. Right now there was only the work for Chigi and His Holiness. He would write to them with his excuses, omitting of course any reference to this new love.

He returned the letter beneath his cloak and started back down the hill. The sun was now in the western skies, and the shops were beginning to open their shutters and resume their trade. He passed them with little interest until he came to the bookbinder's, a small crooked building that appeared ready to pitch chimney first down the hill. He went in with only a half-formed idea of why he was there. A gift. As he appreciated the art of his predecessors, surely she would enjoy the words written by those who had gone before her.

"You wish for something to be bound?" The old man behind the bench was as bent and crooked as his shop, and when he walked he dragged one leg behind him.

"Do you have any volumes already bound? Poetry, perhaps?" The shop was dark, smelling of leather and damp paper. He was beginning to think he would not be successful in a purchase.

But to his surprise the strange little man pulled down a volume from a shelf, and Raffaello went to study it in the light of the doorway. It was a beautiful book covered in calfskin, the title "Canzoniere" embossed on the cover, the pages elaborately decorated and edged with gold. "It was printed in Venezia," said the bookbinder. "It is a fine volume." However, it was not the book's physical beauty that decided Raffaello on its purchase but rather the lines, an homage to Petrarca's true love, Laura. "Love found me defenseless," he read. Do all men in love discover themselves such?

He was still repeating the line to himself when he almost collided with an old acquaintance on the street in front of the shop. "Raffaello! I did not know you were in Firenze!" It had not occurred to him until now that it might be difficult to go into the streets with his love, for he was well known in the city.

He searched his memory for the man's name, remembering without difficulty the name of the man's father, a wealthy merchant who had once commissioned a Madonna. "I have been staying here secretly," Raffaello explained. "I have been in need of rest, and it is quieter here than in Roma."

"Firenze may be quieter than Roma, but it still is not quiet. If you truly desire peace, you should take a villa in the countryside. You are welcome to use mine. I fear business will be keeping me in Firenze this summer."

Raffaello was surprised by the generous offer on the part of a man he scarcely knew and whose name he could not remember. But it was also very tempting. He and his beloved could be alone there for the entire summer should she so wish it. He would paint her, and she could write . . .

"I can see you find the idea attractive," said his acquaintance. "Shall

I tell my staff to expect you? I would consider it a great honor for you to accept. And if you so desire it, I will tell no one of your presence there."

It was with relief that Raffaello finally recalled the man's name just in time to thank him. They stepped to the side of the road to let pass a pair of gaunt horses straining as they pulled a cart loaded with barrels up the hill. "It will not help, my friend, to beat them so," Raffaello chided their owner, who was thrashing their bony haunches with a stout stick. The man glared at Raffaello without acknowledging his comment, although he appeared to let up slightly on the poor animals.

"You have heard, have you not, of Leonardo da Vinci's death?" Raffaello's companion asked as they stepped back into the street and continued down the hill. "The news arrived only yesterday from Paris."

Leonardo dead? Raffaello tried to grasp the importance of the event. "The world has lost a great painter and a great man," he said at last, the words sounding trivial when applied to someone like Leonardo. "And I have lost a great friend and teacher."

He repeated this sentiment later in the little church where he found himself for the second time that day, this time to light a candle and say a prayer for Leonardo's soul. But he had lit them all for her, and the normally dark church was still filled with their smoky glow. He remembered the joy he had felt that led him to light them all, the light-headed, light-hearted joy he still felt. "I dream of our meeting." He wanted to shout out the words in the church.

"Leonardo," he whispered instead. "Please forgive me, my friend. I did not leave a single candle for you. I want to mourn your death, but I fear my happiness will not allow me to do so properly."

Passing by vineyards

How do I love thee? Let me count the ways . . ."
Miss Elizabeth Barrett wrote these famous lines to her lover and soon-to-be husband, Robert Browning, but I will address them to thee, fair Florence! It is of little wonder that these poetic lovers chose to make this city their home; I fear I shall not have the strength to leave myself. The Boboli Gardens, the Ponte Vecchio, the charming streets, the views from the hills—all are an uncountable feast for the senses.

After his beloved wife's death, Robert never again could bring himself to return to Florence. But I visited Elizabeth's grave this morning and left a rose there in his name among the offerings from other pilgrims. Poor Elizabeth. Her father was in violent opposition to the couple's marriage, and he never again spoke to his daughter. Perhaps this rift between parent and child is why Robert in later life endured the many foibles of their only son, "Pen," the sordid tale of which I related to you, dear reader, while in Venice.

The couple's Florentine home, Casa Guidi, located across from the Pitti Palace, has fallen into scandalous disrepair, and one can only hope *it will be rescued before it is turned into the offices of some dreary accounting firm.*

Squawking pigeons shoot into the air and cursing tourists scatter as a red Alfa Romeo convertible, horn blaring, careens into the Piazza della Signoria. Tulia has been sitting on the edge of the fountain reading, but as the car screeches to a halt in front of her, she jumps up and tucks Miss Mercy into her day pack.

"Your chariot awaits, signorina." Raphael lounges casually in the driver's seat wearing a brown leather jacket and aviator sunglasses, his hair pulled back loosely into a ponytail, a boyish grin lighting up his face. He kisses her on both cheeks before pulling off his glasses with a flourish and tossing them into the backseat, which also holds what looks like her suitcases.

"Are those mine?" she asks, climbing in beside him. He presses down on the accelerator before she even has a chance to shut the door, and they are halfway across the piazza by the time she finally tugs it closed.

"I hope you do not mind, but I took the liberty of checking you out of your hotel." Tulia doesn't even ask how he knew what hotel she was staying at, let alone how he found her. "Did you have a nice stay in Firenze?" he asks, looking more at her than at the road.

"Yes," she says over the roar of the engine. Like Miss Mercy, she has seen all the famous sites: the Duomo, the Gates of Paradise, the Ponte Vecchio. She went to the Pitti Palace where she saw Raffaello's *Madonna della Seggiola,* its graceful simplicity a refreshing contrast to the palace's decadence. She liked the palace gardens more than the palace itself, leaving them to climb the hill to the Piazzale Michelango, which didn't exist in Raffaello's time. And of course she has been in the Uffizi, heading straight to the Raffaellos. She studied in particular the artist's self-portrait, the beardless one Raphael mentioned in Paris. With those mournful eyes, the resemblance to her Raphael is so extraordinary that she almost expected to hear him murmur *Eyes like the dawn and the face of an angel* . . .

It was while leaving the Uffizi courtyard where dozens of artists gather to sell their versions of the Florentine landscape that she spotted a small sidewalk painting in a corner of the Piazza della Signoria. Two plump cherubs drifted on delicate cream-colored wings, shooting arrows from drawn bows, a detail from Raffaello's *Galatea*. At last! And so she sat on the fountain's edge and waited for him to find her.

She winces as Raphael barely avoids hitting an old woman carrying a basket filled with vegetables. "Where are we going?"

"To the countryside," he yells as he revs the engine at a stoplight. An arrow points the way to Fiesole. She smells burnt rubber as they roar up the road in a hideous grinding of gears. "Scared, Tulia?" He laughs. "Fear not—this is Italy!" And he revs the engine again.

They race up two-lane roads farther into the Tuscan hills. The scenery whizzes by—verdant vineyards, silvery olive trees, cypresses so dark they seem almost black—but she can't relax enough to enjoy the view.

"Oh, *cara*," he says loudly. "Someday you will become accustomed to Italian driving."

"Well, I do live in New York," she shouts a little indignantly, pushing her wind-whipped hair out of her face. "There's good driving and then there's bad driving."

"Are you saying I do not know how to drive?" He seems hurt, the corners of his mouth exaggeratedly turned down.

"Well, this isn't a Grand Prix," she shouts again, gripping her seat's edge as he swerves past a man on a moped. The man yells expletives at them as they speed away. "Just how long have you been driving?" she asks, not sure she wants to know the answer.

"Since this morning," he says evenly. "I am a fast learner, do you not think so?" And although he starts to laugh again, he eases off the accelerator, and she is finally able to relax. A warm breeze curls across her face.

"I went to Urbino before coming to Florence," she tells him, glad she no longer has to shout.

"Urbino," he says wistfully. "I have not been there in so long. Did you like it?"

"The Ducal Palace is incredible. I saw the house where Raffaello grew up too. I also have a confession to make." From the moment she left the police station, she has been trying to decide whether or not she should tell him.

"What?" He is staring intently at the road.

"I almost turned you over to the Urbino police," she admits.

"The police!" The car swerves onto the side of the road, spitting up gravel. "What did I do?"

"I thought you might be a criminal."

"A criminal?" he says. "Me? How could you think I am a criminal? I am an angel." The car straightens out again.

She laughs. "I'm sorry for being so suspicious, but you can hardly blame me. You're always so mysterious. Like with the plane ticket."

"But that was perfectly logical."

"I know, I know, I believe you. But what have you been doing the last few days?" Her eyes widen. "Oh my God, are you married?" No doubt he has a delightful wife and perfectly charming children somewhere, she thinks. Aren't Europeans notorious for this kind of thing? At least that's the stereotype.

"On this, *cara,* I can give you a definitive answer," he says, half turning to her. "I am not married—I never have been—and there is no place I would rather be than right here." He slows the car down as he points to a tiny village clinging to the hillside. "Caprese. Michelangelo was born there."

"Really? Did you know that he and Raffaello were great rivals?"

"You have been doing your homework, I see. The rivalry was actually rather one-sided. Michelangelo was convinced that everyone was stealing his ideas. The way he went on, you would have thought he invented painting."

"I read that when Michelangelo was painting the Sistine Chapel, Raffaello swiped the keys and went to look at it before it was finished. Michelangelo then claimed Raffaello stole his ideas and put them in his *Sybils* mural."

"That is only rumor," he says firmly. "Everybody influenced everybody else, but Raffaello was one of the few artists to actually own up to it. And Michelangelo was none too pleased that Raffaello was the better painter."

She looks at him. "How do you know they're only rumors?"

As they head up an especially steep grade, he shifts gears, this time much more smoothly. "From so much studying, I guess," he says finally. "Every brushstroke tells a story."

She certainly can't deny that he seems to know Raffaello's works—at least some of them—brushstroke for brushstroke. Or at least chalkstroke.

"Why do you do Raffaellos?" she asks. "Is it because you look so much like him?"

"I do not look like him," he says seriously. "He looks like me."

She laughs. Another typical answer. "Okay then," she says, "who would start such rumors?"

"Most likely it was Giorgio Vasari."

"That's where I got the story about the Sistine Chapel, from Vasari's *Lives of the Artists,*" she says as they fly through the hilltop town of Fiesole. Florence is nestled in the hazy valley below, a sea of red-tiled roofs. "I bought it at a gift shop in Urbino. But why would he write that if it isn't true?"

"Vasari was barely a child when Raffaello died, so he did not know him personally. All the information he got was thirdhand. But as historians have been taking their cues from him ever since, there is still a lot of misinformation about Raffaello."

It hasn't occurred to her to question her sources. What other things has she read that are inaccurate? "Raphael," she asks hopefully, "was the baker's daughter Raffaello's great love?"

"*La fornarina?*" He brakes for some chickens pecking in the gravel on the road. They look up, unconcerned, and return to pecking as he drives carefully around them. "How could you ever believe that? It is just another rumor that got its start in Vasari. She and Raffaello may have been lovers, but she was not his great love."

"I knew it!" She can't believe how relieved this makes her feel. "I kept looking at her portrait, and it just didn't seem right. I couldn't see them as soul mates. And I remember you telling me in Paris that Raffaello never painted his ideal woman. It just didn't add up. It's been bothering me ever since because I thought I was taking too many liberties with history in my book, but maybe not . . ." She breaks off, realizing she has given away her secret, though she supposes her many questions may have already tipped him off.

"Well, now you do not have to worry," he says with a satisfied-looking grin. "So your novel is about Raffaello Sanzio, as I have been suspecting. I guess I am to thank for that."

"I told you that you inspired me." She is not yet ready to tell him how the artist Raffaello will share his story—and lover—with a modern-day sidewalk artist.

"I read your book, *Heaven on Earth,*" he says.

"Where did you ever find that?" She knows it wasn't translated into Italian.

"I wanted to read it," he says. "So I had to find it. It was easier than you think." She is embarrassed but also pleased that he went to such an enormous effort. "I really liked it," he continues. "It was all about *amore*. That is nothing to be ashamed of. And I fell in love with your heroine."

"This one is going to be better," she says, wondering how he'd react if she told him the heroine was based on herself. "In fact, I had another dream in Urbino. But I remembered you telling me not to be afraid. I think it may have helped."

"Magnifico," he says. "You will make more progress now." They pass a field of sunflowers, their enormous yellow and black heads offset by the deepening blue of the afternoon sky. "And any more e-mails from what's-his-name?"

She laughs. "Ethan, you mean. Yes, he sent me a message a few days ago. I didn't answer. But working on this book has certainly helped me keep my mind off him." She doesn't add what she's thinking—*and you have too.*

"Over time," he says, and she strains to hear his voice over the roar of a passing truck, "our lovers become stories we can go back to and remember how they were written. At least, that is the idea. It is important to have courage and move on to the next one."

There is not just one happy ending. She likes this story metaphor and is comforted to know that she has more than one shot at getting it right. But while she is now ready to move on—to put Ethan behind her and start a new story—she is not sure Raphael is very good at following his own advice. What about the woman with the oranges? Where does she fit in? He has not mentioned her again, but Tulia still senses her presence somewhere in his eyes.

Is that what you have done then, moved on? she wants to ask him. Because I'm ready when you are.

But he is looking straight ahead, seemingly lost in his own thoughts. And so, unsure of how he might reply, she stays silent for the rest of the drive.

Where the sun sleeps

Vineyards on the sides of green hills, a flowering garden full of white roses and red poppies, perfectly straight rows of olive trees, brilliant azure skies, and puffy white clouds—all inside the two-story foyer of a Tuscan villa. Tulia has stepped into a painting, an elaborate trompe l'oeil where the flowers are so real she can almost smell them.

"Is this place yours?"

"No, it is borrowed," Raphael replies, guiding her past a sweeping staircase to the back of the room, where doors open up onto a stone terrace. Real pink roses climb the apricot-colored villa wall, and lemon trees grow in terra-cotta planters near the steps to a garden. Farther down, a stream snakes through the valley. No other houses can be seen, and it is so serene, so still and peaceful.

"It's wonderful," she says, sitting down in one of the wrought-iron chairs flanking a round table topped with mosaic. The sun is setting behind the hills, and Raphael lights some torches and candles. "Do you often spend time here?"

"I used to live in Firenze when I studied art. But I have not been back for a long time." He goes inside and returns with a large tray bearing a bottle of Chianti, two glasses, pasta, bread, and a bunch of red grapes in a painted porcelain bowl.

"Did you prepare all this?"

"I have my ways," he says, uncorking the bottle. He pours the wine and hands her a glass. *"Buon appetito,"* he says as he touches his glass to hers.

Aware of how hungry she is, she eagerly accepts a plate of pasta and takes a bite. "Delicious," she says, reaching for a slice of bread. "An artist, a cook, and a very good driver. Once you realized it wasn't a Grand Prix, that is." In the fading light, she can just make out his smile.

By the time they finish their meal, it is truly night. A pale moon has ascended from behind the dark hills, and the first stars have appeared, pinpoints of heaven. She lazily plucks a grape from the bowl while he lights a cigarette.

"I still wonder why Vasari would make up stories about Raffaello's soul mate," she says.

Raphael divides the remainder of the wine between their glasses. "He probably thought it was good detective work on his part. In the last two years of his life, Raffaello was handing more and more of his work, especially at the Vatican, over to his students, and his clients were complaining that he was never around. So Vasari decided there must be a woman distracting him. Not an illogical assumption as the papal court was a fairly promiscuous place. In those days, even the popes had illegitimate children. And to find an artist's mistress, one usually didn't have to look much further than his model. Hence, *la fornarina*. Though why she was considered more special than any of Raffaello's other models, I have no idea. She was not the only one who could have been his lover." He takes a leisurely drag of his cigarette.

"So if Raffaello wasn't spending all of his time with her, what was he doing?"

"He was still painting. The commissions. Portraits of his friends in the court. And there was *The Transfiguration*. He was also busy cataloguing Roman ruins."

"So what you're saying then is that there was no lover. He was just busy."

"I did not say that. Only that there is no mention of a lover in surviving contemporary accounts. But that does not mean he did not love someone. Just that if he did, she has been lost to history."

She takes a sip of wine. "A secret lover," she says with satisfaction. She may be lost to history, but Tulia is bringing her back to life.

"You are giving Raffaello a secret lover in your book then?"

"Yes," she says. And now she hesitates, wondering if she should tell him how much her version of Raffaello's story is based on what he told her about himself. That, in a sense, it is Raphael's story she is writing, not just Raffaello's. But to tell him is to risk hearing that he is still in love with the woman with the oranges. That he could enjoy Tulia's company, even perhaps flirt. But not love her. And that is what she wants, isn't it?

Her mind is almost made up not to say anything when she notices him looking at her. How can she not tell him? He deserves to know. "Raphael," she says. "There's something else." He looks at her expectantly. "I'm using the story you told me as the inspiration for Raffaello's lover. The woman with the oranges."

He doesn't say anything.

"I hope you don't mind," she adds hastily, worried that she has offended him. "If you don't want me to—"

"No," he interrupts. "I do not mind. Write about her. I want you to."

"Are you sure?"

"Absolutely."

"Thank you," she says simply.

The night is soft and quiet. Beyond the glow of the candles, she sees something flicker among the trees. "Look, fireflies. It's like the stars have come down to play for us." It's perhaps a silly thing to say, but she can't help it—she's happy. They sit watching the winking fireflies until he finishes his cigarette and she can't keep her eyes open any longer.

"It is time for bed, *cara*," he says, getting up. "You must be well rested for tomorrow."

He puts his elbow out for her to hook her arm through, and she rests her head on his shoulder. He takes a candle and lights their way through the magically painted foyer and up the stairs. Tired as she is, she is not unaware that she is alone with the man she desires, and she imagines making sleepy love with him, the kind that drifts in and out of dreams.

"This way," he says, pushing open the carved wooden door at the top of the staircase. A window is cracked open to let in the evening air, and she can hear crickets chirping. Gauzy curtains hang from a four-poster bed topped with a canopy. On the covers sits a nightgown trimmed with handcrafted Venetian lace and a sheer shawl.

"Is this to your liking?" he asks, peering at her drooping lids.

"It's perfect." She sits on the edge of the bed, staring up at his velvet eyes. He stands over her. He is going to kiss me, she thinks. But he only lifts her chin with a calloused finger.

"So beautiful," he whispers, inspecting her critically. He runs his finger lightly over her lips. "*Buona notte, bella* Tulia. Tomorrow, I will paint you."

And dreams awake

*B*ellissima," Raphael says. Wearing the sheer gown he gave her the night before, Tulia sits on the chair he has dragged from the villa into the garden. He drapes the shawl over one arm and arranges her hair around her other shoulder. His fingers brush the skin of her throat, and she feels the sweet pain of desire. He gives her a knowing smile. Does he feel it too?

He stands behind the easel placed a few feet away and picks up a brush from the wooden table beside him. It is so quiet. No traffic to be heard, no planes overhead. Only the delicate rustle of leaves, the occasional warble of a songbird, and Raphael's gentle voice.

"Relax," he says. "It is not necessary to be completely still."

She takes a sip of Chianti and gazes out on the sun-filled valley, the dark line of cypress that follows the stream, the hillside opposite with its rows of twisted olive trees. She looks back at him, her eyes meeting his. Can he show what she feels? Will it all be there in his painting?

But she cannot ask, and so she talks to him about Raffaello

instead. "I've been thinking about what you said on the Eiffel Tower, about Raffaello painting from his ideal of a woman. So the women he painted, they weren't models. Maybe they were just his vision of beauty. In which case, the baker's daughter could have been a figment of his imagination."

He laughs softly. "You are very determined to eliminate the poor baker's daughter, are you not? I am beginning to think you are a little jealous of her. Or should I say your secret lover is perhaps a little jealous."

"Raphael, be serious," she says but not too sternly. "Do you think it's possible?"

"It is possible, *cara*. But Raffaello did paint portraits of real people. However, you are also right. Whenever Raffaello painted women, he painted them with his vision of perfection before him. He always hoped to meet a woman who lived up to that ideal. But it was not just an outer physical beauty he sought. It was also a spiritual one."

"That's what makes his Madonnas so special, isn't it?" she says as a butterfly lands momentarily on the easel's edge then flutters away. "Not just that they are beautiful women but that they radiate so much more. Love, I think."

They are silent for a long while as Raphael moves behind the easel. She watches him, their eyes meeting every time he looks over the canvas. She sips at her wine, which has grown warm in the heat of the day, tasting to her of fields and sunshine.

"It is so sad," she says, "that Raffaello may never have met someone he could truly love."

"But he did, *cara*. You are writing about her, are you not?"

She pauses, a little confused. The wine and the heat maybe. She tries to focus her thoughts. The woman with the oranges is real, but she was Raphael's lover, not Raffaello's.

"I'm only making her up based on the story you told me," she says a little uncertainly.

"But what is to say you are not right?" he says, the paintbrush poised in his hand. "Maybe Raffaello really did have a secret lover. You do have good instincts." And he brushes the canvas again. Some of his hair breaks free of its ribbon and falls over one eye. Absently, he pushes it away, leaving a smudge of vermilion on his forehead.

He is so beautiful. He looks up, and she closes her eyes as if to keep him from reading her thoughts. *Do I love him?*

"Tired, *cara?*" he asks. His voice sounds far away, as soft as the breeze through the leaves.

She opens her eyes. "Yes," she whispers, not knowing whose question she is answering.

"Then lie on the grass and inspire me from there," he says.

She complies and stretches out beneath the tree. It is so quiet. *I love him.*

The grass is feathery beneath her, and around her face red poppies sway on delicate stems. She looks up through the leaves of the tree, translucent greens floating on the perfect May sky. A bee drones by her ear and spirals lazily, almost drunkenly, out of sight. She breathes in the scent of grass and flowers and closes her eyes, falling into that place between waking and sleeping where all the dreams reside.

Because it is a dream, isn't it? Conjured by the wine and the sun. Of desire so recently acknowledged. And how can she know for sure if it is not a dream? Powerless as she is to break the spell by opening her eyes.

She feels it again. Surely it is only the brush of petals against her lips, only the whisper of the breeze against her hair, the touch of grass against her thigh. And what else could it be but the sun, caught beneath the fabric of her gown, caressing her skin with its warmth?

The ground drops away from her and she is floating, the earth dissolving beneath her, weightless in an azure Italian afternoon.

Are you there? She does not speak aloud; there is no need for speech in dreams.

I am here, cara. *You are not afraid, are you?*

Not with you. You won't leave me, will you?

I will always be with you. Sleep, cara, *sleep.*

And she is asleep, isn't she? And if she hears music, it is only the wind playing in the branches of the trees. Only the sun that wraps her in its rays and fills her body with light. And maybe it is only the velvety poppies that kiss her lips. But she knows now what it must be like to touch heaven.

Beneath Italian skies

"Raphael, how old are those olive trees?"

"No hello? Just more questions?" He kisses Tulia on the cheek and sets the glass of rusty-colored Cinzano on the table. He has been working all morning in the stone outbuilding he calls his studio, and a tiny spot of red paint like blood mars the back of his hand. She closes Vasari's *Lives of the Artists* and places it on top of her notebook.

He pulls up a chair, the legs scraping across the stone terrace. "I suppose next you will want to know why the sky is blue."

No, but she would like to know where the ice cubes in her drink come from when the villa doesn't have a refrigerator, let alone a freezer. But she doesn't ask. She is coming to expect these things of Raphael, these small miracles. *If I told you it would not be magic,* he said to her centuries ago on a sidewalk in Paris. So long as he doesn't disappear in a puff of smoke, so long as this isn't only an illusion, she will happily believe in magic.

He settles into his chair, sipping his drink and looking at the shimmer of olive trees. "They can live for two thousand years. So technically they could have been there since the birth of Christ, but more likely they were planted when the villa was built." He does not mean "their" villa but rather the villa just out of view over the hilltop. "So five hundred years, give or take a decade or two."

"Then they could have been planted already when Raffaello was here."

He looks over at her. "Raffaello was here? At this villa? How do you know that?"

She shrugs. "I don't," she says. "But it isn't impossible." She is continually faced with decisions like this as she tries to fill in the blanks of Raffaello's life. And so she can't help but think that, if not exactly here, Raffaello and his lover must have spent time very much like this in a place very much like this.

Raphael agrees it is not impossible. He even suggests that perhaps the stone outbuilding where he has been working on her portrait these past two weeks could have been Raffaello's studio. Even the birthplace of *The Transfiguration*.

"But not his lover's portrait?"

"Ah," he says slowly, "but I thought she was a secret lover."

"Yes, but he was Raffaello. He loved to paint women. How could he not paint the woman he loved?"

"It does not matter how much he loved her," he says adamantly. "If he painted her, then she would not have stayed a secret."

Tulia considers this. She wants Raffaello to have painted his lover, just the way Raphael is painting her. She wants them to have made love, just as she and Raphael first did under the brilliant Tuscan sun. Fulfillment so exquisite, as if she had been waiting for it forever. She felt taken out of herself, to some place beyond her body, beyond the earth.

"With or without the painting," she says, "he couldn't have kept her a complete secret. There would have been servants."

"But servants would not have recorded her presence. And

speaking of servants, how did Raffaello's lover get here from Roma?" He goes on to tell her he cannot imagine Raffaello letting his beloved travel with only a servant as company—the roads were too dangerous. Thieves and highwaymen hid out in the under-brush, ready to ambush travelers. Escaping with one's life was for-tunate, though being left stranded in the countryside meant one was at the mercy of strangers, not always friendly. Of course, at-tempts were made to curtail the highwaymen. Perpetrators' bod-ies were often left hanging by the road as a warning to other bandits and to reassure travelers.

Tulia can't imagine this being much comfort, but she feels cer-tain that Raffaello's lover came here to meet him and so suggests that Raffaello would have hired men to accompany her. Armed men, Raphael stresses. Fine, she says, I'll change it to armed men. But the problem of the portrait still bothers her. Raffaello had met his muse. Of course he would want to paint her.

"He may have wanted to, but he did not actually do so," Raphael insists. "Besides, if he had, where is that portrait today? It is not in the Uffizi or anywhere else."

"I don't know," she answers with frustration, watching a pink petal float down from where the roses climb high up the villa wall. "Maybe it was destroyed in a fire or something. I'm not suggesting this really happened, Raphael. Walking this line between fact and fiction is confusing. For example, the only evidence I have of a se-cret lover is that there is no contemporary mention of such a lover. So if she existed, she was kept secret and nobody will ever know who she was."

"Nobody will ever know who she was because he did not paint her."

He is so insistent that she finally just laughs. "Okay, I give up. Raffaello didn't paint his lover. Much as I would have liked him to." She kisses him on the cheek. "But somehow I think he would have let her see her portrait and not be mean like yourself, painting every day in the studio, and keeping me in terrible suspense."

Raphael just smiles and goes back to talking about olive trees. She sips at her drink and only half listens. She is picturing Raffaello and his lover sitting here on the same terrace, looking out over the same olive grove, but newly planted. They would talk about writing, art, politics, philosophy . . . maybe even olive trees . . .

That is how it has been these last few weeks. Just as she writes the details of the days Raffaello and his beloved spent together, she is also documenting her own time with Raphael. And so she writes how Raffaello and his beloved awoke every morning in the four-poster bed she now shares with Raphael, their limbs entwined beneath the sheets. The cool morning breeze infused with the scent of roses lifting the lace curtains. Making love in the soft light of the rising sun. They would drink coffee . . . no, not coffee, she thinks, it will be close to another century before coffee is introduced to Italy . . . well, drink *something* here on the terrace. Raffaello would spend his mornings in the studio, while his beloved would sit on the terrace writing. Just as Tulia does now. The sun shining all the time. The same sun that shines now.

"You are not listening to a word I am saying, are you?"

She returns to the present. Not with a jolt, but with that happiness she feels when she awakes to find Raphael beside her and knows he isn't a dream but real. "I was listening," she says. "Although maybe not to your words."

He laughs. "There will be a test on this later, but first I will make us some lunch, as you Americans call it."

She follows him into the kitchen, resting against one of the marble-topped wooden cupboards, the stone cool through her linen shirt. She has brought her glass of Cinzano and sets it down beside her.

She loves this kitchen, even with or maybe because of the complete lack of modern appliances. It is a large room with a stone floor, beamed ceiling, and whitewashed walls stained with years of smoke from the gargantuan stone fireplace that makes up almost one entire wall. Raphael uses the hand pump in the copper sink to wash the fresh tomatoes and sprays of basil, setting them out on the long harvest table in front of the fireplace. She chooses two white porcelain plates with painted yellow rims from one of the open shelves, wipes them with a towel, and sets them on the table. This is all the work he will allow her, insisting that she is on vacation. And so she has turned it into a ritual, choosing each day between the different gaily hand-painted plates and the more somber pewter ones.

He slices the tomatoes onto the dishes, then takes out a small round ball of fresh mozzarella from the cupboard that is her post. Where does all this wonderful food come from? Perhaps someone comes to the door each morning while she is still asleep, bringing warm eggs, crusty bread, and vegetables like these tomatoes that smell like summer and have so clearly never darkened the door of a supermarket. Or maybe Raphael steals out to some nearby market when she thinks he is working in his studio, smuggling back all this good food—and ice cubes too.

After cutting the mozzarella, he arranges it among the tomatoes. Next is the basil and, over it all, a fine stream of olive oil. *"Prego,"* he says, handing her the plates. *"Insalata caprese. Semplice ma molto deliziosa."*

He follows her back out onto the terrace carrying a round country loaf and the inevitable bottles of wine and mineral water. The sun is high now, and they move the table into the shade of what she calls a sycamore and what he calls a plane tree, disturbing two little lizards that scurry across the terrace and disappear between a crack in the stones. They sit not across from each other but at right angles, affording them both a view of the valley and the added advantage of closeness.

"This is so good," she says, starting in on her salad. "Like everything else you've made me. I don't think I've ever enjoyed food so much."

He saws off a slice of bread and hands it to her. "It is the fresh air."

They eat in silence for a few minutes before she picks up the thread of their earlier conversation. "Let me play devil's advocate for a moment. What if Raffaello didn't have a lover at all? Secret or otherwise. Since there's no contemporary mention, it may be the most logical conclusion of all." She takes a sip of water, having turned down the wine. She is beginning to think she shouldn't drink wine with every meal. It is the sort of behavior one is warned about in television commercials, the slippery slope to alcoholism.

Raphael looks up. "What, Raffaello not have a lover? You mean he was celibate? No one at all?"

"You sound so incredulous."

"You have seen his portrait. Is he not, as they say today, 'hot'?"

She laughs and decides to have the glass of wine after all. She will worry about alcoholism later. "Okay then, maybe he was gay. My friend Jasmine is always saying that all the good-looking men are gay." She sets the bottle back down on the table. How easily and naturally she said "my friend Jasmine," as if nothing has come between them. Her life back in New York is beginning to seem as though it happened to someone else.

"So your friend would not think I am good-looking?" Raphael asks.

"I'm beginning to think you're very vain," she says, shaking her fork at him.

He leans across the table and kisses her playfully on the tip of her nose. "It is a weakness of Italian men."

"So then you *are* Italian, not French," she says, triumphant in having inadvertently made him confess this one small clue to his identity.

He laughs, unfazed. "I did not say that. I was only saying that Italian men are vain. I am not. So do not look so pleased with yourself. Like the canary that got the cream," he says, this time kissing her on the mouth.

"Don't think you can distract me with kisses," she says, spearing the last tomato. "I caught you. You're slipping, Raphael. And it's the cat, not the canary, that got the cream. Although the cat also got the canary."

He mutters something about the inanity of the English language as they take their dishes back to the kitchen. Raffaello was not gay, he tells her quite seriously as he starts to wash the plates and glasses. You can see from both Michelangelo's and Leonardo's paintings how people might conclude they were gay, and it is almost certain Leonardo was. But Raffaello doesn't share Michelangelo's passion for the male body, and his portraits of women don't contain the irony seen in Leonardo's *Mona Lisa.*

Leaving him to finish cleaning up the kitchen, she goes to collect their towels and the big quilt from their bed. Resting on the bedside table is the book on Raffaello she bought at the Louvre. She takes it to the window and, laying it on the sill, opens it to the page with *La Madonna della Seggiola,* the painting she went to see at the Pitti Palace in Florence. A peasant woman with a simple headdress of striped browns sits on a wooden chair; only a richly decorated sleeve indicates that she is no ordinary peasant. The Christ child, plump, more childlike than divine, curled up in the safety of his mother's arms, looks out at the viewer with distrust. She remembers Caroline's and Matthew's quest for the homeliest depiction of the Christ child. Had their quest been instead for the loveliest, this might have been it. At least it is her favorite.

And then there is the Madonna herself. No heavenward look of religious piety. She may be the Madonna, but she is a woman first, and the painter is won over by her femininity and loveliness. Raphael is right. Her gaze is not one that would puzzle art historians for years, like the *Mona Lisa*. It is only a look of simple, unabashed love. But for whom? God? The painter?

Underneath the picture is a quotation by Picasso—*Da Vinci promises heaven, but Raffaello, he gives it to us*—and she suddenly thinks that in this comparison to the *Mona Lisa* she may have solved something else. There is a reason Leonardo and Michelangelo have since stolen the limelight from Raffaello, why so many more books are devoted to them. Raffaello is too gentle for the modern world, too sincere for a time that thrives on ironies.

She puts the book away and goes back downstairs with the towels and quilt to where Raphael waits for her on the terrace. He is smoking a cigarette, his back to the door, looking out over the valley below, a golden shimmer in the heat of the afternoon. He wears his black jeans and a loose white shirt. His hair flows around his shoulders, and a canvas bag is slung over one arm. She pauses in the doorway, watching him. When he turns to her, his face is serious, lined with a weariness she sees sometimes when he doesn't know she is watching. Wanting to reassure him, she takes a step forward. But before she can ask what troubles him, the look dissolves into a lazy smile, and she soon forgets it was ever there.

They do not have to discuss where they are going, for this too is part of their daily ritual. Holding hands, they walk down the path through the garden that leads them to the hot spring flowing from the hills. She wonders how soon before poppies sprout from the seeds she scattered here, the ones she gathered from the botanical gardens in Paris. She likes the idea of leaving something behind to mark her happiness.

It is so quiet that she can separate and identify all the sounds.

Their soft footsteps on the dirt, the distant call of a cuckoo, and, as they approach it, the rush of the waterfall. She has never experienced silence like this. Not even at her parents' cabin in the mountains, where the noises of the modern world always encroached. Radios, motorboats, a plane overhead, a neighbor's chain saw or lawn mower. Certainly peaceful compared with the city, but not like this, where the quiet is a soft embrace.

Water cascades down white rocks into a circular, chest-deep pool edged with great squared stones that Raphael has told her were put in place by the ancient Romans. They built other structures here too, and while they are long gone, he showed her the slight rise that marks the remains of a foundation.

Tulia spreads the quilt on the grass in a nearby copse of sycamores. She takes the book of Petrarch sonnets he has given her, written in Italian with English translations on the opposite pages, and laughs when she sees what he has brought for himself. "Miss Mercy? I can't believe you're reading that, Raphael."

"Why not? I am learning a lot."

"It's a bit over the top, don't you think? I'm only reading it because my father gave it to me as a going-away present. Its style perfectly epitomizes what my parents are like."

"And how is that?"

"Out of touch with the modern world. They've been that way my whole life."

"What is wrong with that? There is a certain charm in being a little out of touch—like Miss Mercy. It is just a different way of seeing the world."

"Maybe. But I just wish they had made a little more effort to relate to me. They never seemed to want me around. It's like I messed up their perfect little academic world with my unexpected arrival."

"Are you really sure you were not wanted? Not everyone is good at communicating how they feel. Perhaps they even feel rejected by you."

"I've never considered that before." All this time she has felt unwanted, and maybe they've also been thinking how ungrateful she is. Embarrassed by their ages. And always wanting to leave home. She was absolutely gleeful to leave them for New York. But isn't it a parent's job to make their children feel wanted?

"Perhaps you are a little hard on them. Everything in your life has brought you to this point, lying here under these trees with me. Would you want it any different?" he asks, pulling her into his arms.

"Of course not," she says, kissing him.

"Have you tried telling them how you feel? I am sure you will find them more receptive than you think. It is time to forgive them and appreciate that they are still with you."

"And your parents are not?" she asks tentatively.

"I only knew them for a little while."

"I'm sorry," she says contritely, knowing she has learned a little more about him. "You're probably right. Maybe I'm being too hard on them. They certainly were never malicious. And perhaps in their own odd ways they really do mean well."

"So are you going to let me read you Miss Mercy?"

She nestles in his arms in response.

"O glorious Petrarch, I do hope that you are not in Heaven laughing at an old woman's pitiful efforts to pay you homage by traveling to the place of your birth. Arezzo—birthplace not only of the father of humanism but also the biographer and artist Giorgio Vasari. Unable to unravel the mysteries of the local bus routes, I found myself and my luggage some miles from my intended destination. Goodness knows what would have befallen me had a local man not come to my aid. A

charming man, a widower who has retired in much comfort among the vineyards his family has tended for generations . . ."

Tulia laughs. "I bet anything she sat on her suitcase, pulled out her knitting, and put out her thumb every time a car passed."

"No," Raphael says. "I think her charming widower rode a scooter."

"But she would've had to put her knitting away. Not even Miss Mercy could knit on the back of a scooter."

"I would not be so sure," he says, then picks up reading from where he left off.

"But on to Francesco Petrarch, the reason for my pains. It is impossible to speak of Francesco without first mentioning Laura, his muse. While history still debates her existence, I have no doubt that she was real. From the day he glimpsed her on the steps of the church in Avignon, France, in 1327, he loved her. But did she even know of his adoration? Or, knowing it, did she simply not return his affections? She was, after all, married to another. To this great unrequited love, Francesco wrote hundreds of poems, and when Laura died on Good Friday, exactly twenty-one years after the day he first laid eyes on her, he wrote of her death with deep sorrow."

Good Friday, Tulia thinks. The same day Raffaello was born and died. Raphael reads on, and she finds herself listening not just to the words but also to the cadence of his voice.

"Perhaps," he says when he finishes, "you can write about Laura one day. Once you solve the mystery of Raffaello's beloved, of course." He closes the book. "Enough Miss Mercy for today," he says as he opens her Petrarch volume. He reads a sonnet aloud to her in the Italian, the words like music, while she follows along in English.

O what fear when I recall the day
I left my love, grave and thoughtful,
and my heart with her! Nothing else
do I think of so often . . .

Afterward they shed their clothes, leaving them scattered on
the quilt. Tulia climbs into the pool by the waterfall. She stands beneath the flow of warm, milky-colored water and closes her eyes,
letting it stream over her face, neck, shoulders. To think that just
over a month ago she was enduring the dregs of another New York
winter, fighting with Ethan, unable to write, unhappy.

When she opens her eyes, she sees Raphael watching her
through the veil of water. She swims toward him, and they float
side by side on their backs. The sky has never been so close or so
big, a cloudless sapphire sea without even a jet trail to break the
endless blue.

And then it happens. A moment of certainty that she—
Raffaello's beloved—was here, immersed in the same sky, her lover
at her side. It is as if Tulia is seeing the sky through the eyes of this
woman she has created. And she knows too how she felt, being
with the man she loved.

But something feels wrong too, horribly wrong. Her dream
comes rushing back with all its terror and desolation, and Tulia
knows with utter certainty that something horrific will happen.

Suddenly she is no longer floating but struggling to find her
footing on the bottom of the pool, inhaling water, darkness flowing over her, heart pounding. *My God, I'm going to drown. Just when
I'm happy, I'm going to die.*

But as quickly as it began, it's over. She is in Raphael's arms,
gasping for air. "Just breathe slowly," he says as he holds her
tightly, smoothing her wet hair. "Everything is fine." He whispers

soothing words until her breathing returns to normal. Helping her out of the pool, he leads her to the quilt, where they lie down together. She rests her head on his chest, and he places his arm around her.

"I'm sorry," she says finally.

"There is nothing to be sorry about," he says, his eyes wide. "Something frightened you. What was it? What happened?"

She can feel the rhythmic beating of his heart. "I was looking up into the sky, thinking how peaceful it was. Then I must have fallen asleep, because all of a sudden I was convinced they were here—Raffaello and his lover. Not just as characters in my book, but for real. I was even looking at the sky through her eyes. But then it became dark like when I first had my dream, and I was afraid. I don't know why—I didn't see anything. Just blackness opening up in front of me. I guess I panicked and started to sink."

"It is all over now," he says. "Everything is going to be fine." And she wants to believe him. With his arm around her, her cheek against his chest, it is hard not to. She turns her head and looks up just as a cuckoo flits through the branches. *They were here.* But how can she be so sure of something she can't possibly know? And how does she know that something awful is about to happen?

She closes her eyes and listens to the streaming waterfall and Raphael's steady breathing. Is this strange experience the result of transferring her fears for her own future onto Raffaello's beloved? Do other writers dream themselves into their novels? Or is this what her book has always been about—her and the sidewalk artist?

These past weeks with Raphael have been the happiest she has ever known, but they never talk of the future. She has told herself this doesn't matter, that she will live simply in the present. But she is fearful about what may happen. Being here in heaven—who would ever want to leave?

She has not asked him before, but now she has to know. "Do you love me, Raphael?" she asks. But only the cuckoo answers. Raphael is already asleep.

Not soon shall I forget
the day

I never know when it will happen or how it will start. I can almost re- member every time, and every time it begins differently. The first time I was very young. We had gone to the villa my father owned outside Venezia. It was summer and very hot, and I was playing in the brook that ran through the villa gardens. I remember how soft the mossy pebbles felt beneath my bare feet. The brook was fed from a spring that never dried up, and the water was cool and fresh. I was holding up my dress so that it would not get wet and watching as tiny fish darted between my ankles. Then I heard the cuckoo."

They lay in the shade of a plane tree, their clothes heaped on the ground beside them, looking up through the sunlit leaves that triggered this mem- ory of hers. It was unusually hot, even for early June, and Raffaello thought that if ever he were to paint leaves so green, a sky so blue, it would never be believed. They came here almost every afternoon to bathe in the spring fed from deep in the earth, warm and milky with minerals, to make love beneath the branches of the trees, to sleep. The ancient Romans knew of this place and had built a bathhouse over the spring. Not much re- mained, but one could still make out the crumbling brick wall and the stone floor with its remnants of mosaic. He had no doubt that the relics had been pillaged and sold as garden decorations; the statues in the villa garden probably came from here. It upset him—he feared their loss to history—and it was why he had begun to catalogue the ruins of Roma. But he was not thinking about any of this at the moment, only listening to her story and the dreamy sound of her voice.

"I looked up," she continued, "trying to find the cuckoo. It sounded so close. And that is when it happened. The sun was filtering through the green leaves, and I thought it was the most exquisite green, perhaps the most exquisite color I had ever seen. But it was not only about being swept away by the beauty; it was also about the realness, the uniqueness, of the moment. For a long second I felt so absolutely and consciously alive. Overwhelmed by the miracle that I was here, now. That an infinite number of probabilities more numerous than the stars had come together so that I should be in this place at this time. It is not that I could have described then what I was feeling. But it was so powerful that I still remember it vividly. I think it was the absolute and awe-inspiring wonder of the miracle of being alive, the absolute and awe-inspiring certainty of our mortality."

He felt this too, but he had never tried to put it in words. Words were not his strong point, as his efforts of the past week reminded him . . .

Amore, you caught me in your net with light
From eyes so bright wherein I melt like snow
Falling a splend'rous white on roses at dusk . . .

Among his sketches he had hidden the lines—so inadequate they were to describe his love for her.

"You forget," he said, "that there is an eternity in the kingdom of heaven."

"Do you truly believe that?" He felt her eyes on him, wide and serious. "What if this is all there is? Sometimes I cannot help but think it is all simply to appease us for our sufferings. So that we bear them quietly."

He could not objectively answer her, not then, with her at his side, with all the misery of the world too distant to be real. He could only whisper something about this being enough—that he could only hope it was in heaven as it was on earth, with her in his arms. He drew her toward him, and they made love again.

Later, in the stone outbuilding he used as his studio, the door open to the afternoon light, he did try to answer her question. It did not take him long to conclude that perhaps it was not a question "the pope's favorite artist," as she once had called him, should even entertain unless he wished his title to change from favorite artist to heretic. And he must warn her too, that while this was an age of new ideas, the old ones were not about to relinquish their power without a fight. Love, he thought, had taught him fear. He could not imagine his life without her.

He turned back to the canvas, a depiction of the greatest miracle—the transfiguration of Christ. It was only in its beginning stages, but he already knew it would be one of his best. He had first envisioned it after seeing Titian's Assumption of the Virgin. *What would Michelangelo make of that? he wondered. Would Michelangelo accuse him of stealing from Titian, or did Michelangelo believe that only his own ideas were worthy of theft? No doubt the latter.*

In Titian's painting, the Virgin ascended heavenward, borne by angels on a cloud toward a light so golden and radiant one's imagination could not begin to conceive of the glories that awaited her. But in that painting, the faces of the onlookers were in shadow, their backs turned to the viewer. This frustrated him. He wanted to see them, to look into their faces and know how this miracle moved them.

On his own canvas it was Christ who ascended heavenward. But these onlookers were not superfluous. He painted their faces, in every one a story, a lifetime of pain, happiness, futility, hope. They did not all, like Titian's, look heavenward. And perhaps that was the message of the age—for despite the promise of Christ's resurrection, he had to admit, it was earthly matters that concerned man most.

He did not work quickly. This time of thought and reflection was as important as the time spent painting. He no longer had the desire to produce endless versions of the Madonna and child for rich patrons. Let Isabelle d'Este find another painter to work for her. For her goal was only to possess something by him for her collection. It was about status and greed, and she would show off his work without a moment's appreciation for it beyond how its possession would instill envy in the hearts of her acquaintances. It angered and saddened him to see his work so cheapened.

He had not learned this attitude during his apprenticeship. Perugino lived with brush in hand, working at a maniacal pace, unwilling to waste a moment of the day, loath to disappoint a patron. "Serve up the soup while I put in another saint," he would call to his wife. He was hungry for money too, keeping all he owned on his person at all times. He spent only with great reluctance, and it was a wonder his wife had anything at all with which to make soup. Despite these failings, Raffaello was grateful to his master, not only for becoming a second father to him but also for the skills he taught him. For the gentle gracefulness that shaped his figures. He did not think anyone could have taught him better, and his love and respect for Perugino were endless.

But Raffaello also desired to move beyond skill into a place where his work transcended paint and canvas. And perhaps that answered her question—what if this was all there was? He knew that beyond himself existed a power he could not explain with reason. He knew it from those moments that she described by the hot spring, and he knew it as his brush moved over the canvas. That was why he painted. Not just to line up the saints on the canvas like so many ninepins. Almost anybody with skill could do that. But rather to capture the divinity in everything he saw around him. To put in each Madonna the love of every woman for her child. He wanted to look into their eyes and find heaven. For that he asked for grace, and often he felt his prayers were answered.

He painted until he lost the light from the door and shadows passed over his canvas. Putting down his brushes, he went in search of his apprentice,

Ugo, to come and clean them. The boy was only nine, and while he already showed signs of having a real gift, he was also sickly. Raffaello had sent for him from Firenze, thinking the country air would serve him well. And apparently it had, for Raffaello found him engaged in somersaulting down the incline near the villa garden to the valley below. The boy, face flushed and eyes full of mischief, came scurrying back up the hill when his name was called, and he ran off toward the studio as quickly as his skinny legs would carry him.

Raffaello found her seated on the terrace. She worked here every day, and it was here they discussed her work. He desired to publish it immediately, but she had made him promise to wait. She wanted a year in which to develop something new, a poem exploring the feminine divine, and he had promised, as he promised her everything. He stood quietly, watching her for a moment. She was wearing a gown, almost ancient Roman in its simplicity, loose and airy, fashioned from natural linen. She had made it herself and was grateful to be able to wear it here; it would be scandalous in modern Roma. Who decided we must wear clothes so unsuited to our climate? she had asked him. Tight bodices, heavy skirts. He didn't have an answer, but following her lead, he had adopted the simple clothes of the local farmers, dreading the return to the costume befitting his position in the papal court.

A sheet of paper weighted with a rock lay on the table in front of her, the late-afternoon breeze just lifting the edge, inkstand and quill beside it. The volume of Petrarca sonnets he had given her lay open in her hands. But she wasn't writing or reading, only looking out over the valley filled with golden light. At the cypresses that lined the stream and the newly planted olive trees on the opposite hillside.

As if sensing his presence, she turned to him, her blue eyes quiet and smiling. "Come," she said, patting the seat of the chair beside her. "You are always working." She went into the house and returned with wine, pouring it into plain pewter cups.

"How is your work coming?" she asked. "I have not been working at all, only daydreaming."

"About what?"

"About how wonderful it would be to stay here forever."

"We can."

"No. I cannot deprive the pope of his favorite painter."

"Earlier you were questioning the existence of heaven, and now you are putting His Holiness's wishes above your own."

"I may question many things. But that does not mean I do not understand how the world is ordered."

Although this was not the answer he wished to hear, she was of course absolutely right, and it did put his mind to rest on another front. He did not suggest that she stay here while he returned to Roma; he could not bear to have her so far away. Besides, it was not always peaceful here. Only days before her arrival, the valley just downstream had been filled with the tents of a mercenary army, perhaps five hundred men plus their women. They were few for such an army, and rumor had it they had split from their regiment in a disagreement over spoils of some battle and were now marching to Milano. They had swept through the countryside, looting and burning farms along the way. His servants had kept watch at night, but had the soldiers decided to overrun the villa, they could have done little to stop them. Miraculously, the soldiers had stayed in their camp, enjoying the plunder of some unfortunate farmer's wine cellar. They drank all the time, hunting during the day and fighting among themselves at night as the women danced in the light of the fires. Then, as abruptly as they came, they left. Raffaello had gone down into the valley with his servants after their departure, and they had burned the half-eaten corpses of deer and boar and buried the body of a man who had died from a dagger to the back.

Raffaello did not tell her any of this, not wanting to spoil this view for her. And it did seem unbelievable, looking out over it now, that it had ever known any violence.

"Then if we cannot stay here forever, let me paint you." He had asked her this before, and he suspected her answer would be the same. But at this moment he desired more than ever to paint her—to immortalize her.

"*You are very insistent. But I do not think the two subjects are related. The answer is still no. You promised me our love would be kept secret.*"

"*Then we will keep the painting a secret,*" he pressed. *He had never wanted to paint anyone as much.*

"*It cannot always be a secret, for your works will outlive us. I do not want history speculating on the identity of the subject or her relationship to the painter. At best, I would be dismissed as just another one of your many models. But given the reputation that painters, yourself included, have for bedding their models, I might as well be thought of as your whore.*"

Her choice of words angered him. "*Will that matter after we are gone? Especially since you question the afterlife.*" *He was grasping at straws. He knew she would never capitulate. He had already learned to recognize that tone in her voice. Always calm, always soft, this gentle surface masking the rock-solid conviction underneath.*

"*It will matter to me, for whether or not there is a heaven, I somehow feel that I would know. Let history speculate on your relationships with your other models, like the one in* La Madonna della Seggiola. *Let historians believe she was your lover. Or la fornarina. I am sure she will cause much speculation. They can write a very sentimental story. About how you loved her but could not marry her as she was only a simple baker's daughter with no dowry, while you were a member of Pope Leo's court.*"

He arose abruptly from the table and went to stand by the terrace's low wall. He had no words for her. For they were not talking about la fornarina. They were talking about themselves. How he could no more marry her than he could la fornarina—as fond as he had been of the baker's daughter, nothing in their relationship had tempted him to defy convention.

He had come a long way from his childhood in Urbino. But along with the privilege came responsibilities and certain expectations. Lovers were one thing, but marriage was different. It was about favors, business partnerships, heirs. If love entered into it, all the better, but it was not essential. He had been betrothed once to Maria Bibbiena, the cardinal's niece. Her death had saddened him, and he mourned her passing, but more for her uncle's sake than his own. And as a sign of respect for his friend, he would be buried next to her.

Should a patron of his suggest he marry one of their daughters now, he would be remiss to say no. Would they continue being lovers then? He did not think her pride would allow it. There was also His Holiness's suggestion that he be made cardinal as a reward for his services, putting an end to the idea of marrying at all. Could he leave the court and tell the pope to find another painter? He was not poor. He had enough money for them to live out their lives comfortably, and for one moment he even had the irrational idea of fleeing to this New World so recently discovered. But one did not go lightly into His Holiness's service, let alone tell God's representative on earth to find himself another painter.

He felt the soft touch of her hand on his arm. "It is all right," she said. "I know the order of things. How they must be. Just do not ask to paint me again. If I am to be remembered, let it be for what I write, not as your mistress."

He held her then. Given that he could not marry her, he never should have fallen in love with her or let her fall in love with him. From now on he was her patron and lover only. He vowed there and then never to say "I love you." To do so would only be selfish.

To: Ethan
From: Tulia
Subject: Re: Re: Re: **I almost forgot**

Dear Ethan,

Greetings from Rome. I hope you and Jasmine are well. I'm still having an amazing time here in Europe. I've been doing lots of research on my new book, and it's going very well.

But that's not what I really want to write about. Ethan, we both know it isn't working anymore. It's the sad truth. We've been going through the motions for quite a while. Things aren't like they were at the beginning. I've been frustrated by my writing, and you've spent all your time on your job. Neither of us has invested much time in our relationship lately. In fact, just before you gave me this trip for my birthday, I was about to break it off. I changed my mind when you said you wanted things to be right between us again. I even went along with your idea that spending time apart would help. I didn't agree with it, but you seemed so convinced this was the solution.

Now, of course, I realize you had another motive for encouraging me to come alone. And at first I was angry. I felt betrayed by both of you. My boyfriend and my good friend. The least you could have done was be honest with me. After the four years we've been together.

But, over the last month, I've come to realize that you and I are not meant to be after all. And I have indeed come to see what a good idea my coming to Europe alone has been.

You may be wondering if there is "someone else." As I want to be more honest with you than you were with me, the short answer is—yes. And he is wonderful, though he is not the reason I am writing this note. It's simply best that you and I move on.

Anyway, that's all I really wanted to say. Maybe, sometime, we can get together for a drink.

Take care,

Tulia

Send

How I wept as I remembered

Raffaello is there as she knew he would be, looking out of one corner among the geometry scholars. The first time she heard of *The School of Athens,* she was at the top of the Eiffel Tower. Almost a lifetime ago. It's hard to believe there was ever a time that she did not know of its existence. The loggia Raffaello painted for Pope Julius, the intricate tapestries he designed for the Sistine Chapel, the culminating achievement of *The Transfiguration*—they're all here. How much she has learned about the Renaissance master in only six weeks—enough to sense his very presence within the walls of these historic buildings. She wouldn't be surprised to turn and see him standing at her side.

But when she does turn, not even Raphael is there. She scans the crowded room, not moving from in front of the painting, sure he will return. But minutes pass and she assumes he has gone on without her. However, he is not in the next room, or the next one either, and it is not until she emerges into sunlight that she sees him.

"That was fast," he says without smiling, dropping the end of his cigarette to the ground.

His words sound like an admonishment, and she is suddenly angry. "Where were you? I was worried."

"Worried? There was no need to worry. I have seen it all before."

"Well, you could have told me you were leaving. I turned around and you were gone. Besides, you're the one who wanted to come here." She wishes they had never come to Rome. Ever since they left the villa, she has had the feeling that he is slipping away from her. He is distracted, and that sadness and weariness she has glimpsed in him before seems ever present. He doesn't even try to hide it anymore.

She wants desperately to ask him again whether he loves her. But she is afraid of his answer. That day by the hot spring, was he really asleep? Did she scare him off by even asking? Is this why they left so unexpectedly? For she awoke the next morning to find her bags neatly packed and Raphael waiting patiently for her on the terrace, foamy cappuccinos on the mosaic table. "It is time to go to Raffaello's city," he said. "You cannot write about Raffaello without visiting Roma." Maybe, but at the villa they were happy. In Rome, she is not so sure.

She starts walking away, even though she does not know where she is going, not even knowing if he will follow her. The sun is relentless, and the heat from the stones of the square emanates through the soles of her sandals.

After only a few steps, he is beside her again. "I am sorry, *cara*. It must be the heat. Please do not be angry with me. Let me take you to see the *Galatea*."

"And you won't leave me?" she asks, the words loaded with more meaning than she intends.

He takes her hand and raises it to his lips. "I will always be with you," he says into her palm, and although she worries he is being deliberately noncommittal, the words have a comforting echo.

Her hand still in his, they walk down the street named Lungotevere Raffaello Sanzio to the vine-covered walls of Trastevere. She likes the lines of laundry stretched above the streets and the purple and red flowers that spill down the brown stone walls. It is cooler here, and she begins to feel a little better as they approach the Villa Farnesina.

While almost disconcertingly quiet, Raphael is true to his promise and does not leave her side as she studies the *Galatea* fresco. Its dreamy goddess rising from the sea, dolphins leaping playfully at her feet, chubby cherubs hovering around her—the same cherubs Raphael reproduced five hundred years later on a sidewalk in Florence.

They pass over the muddy Tiber River to reach the heart of ancient Rome. There they climb Palatine Hill and look out over the remains of the Circus Maximus, where chariot races were once held. Raphael holds her as the fiery sun sinks before them, its dying rays entwining the hills with a violet ribbon of light. He recites:

> "I wept as I remembered
> How often you and I
> Had tired the sun with talking
> And sent him down the sky."

"That's lovely," Tulia says. A breeze whispers through the orange trees, while below them Rome, seemingly peaceful at the end of the day, slips like a sigh into the dusky shadows.

"Callimachus," he offers by way of explanation. She repeats the words to herself, struck this time by the loss in the lines, and although he kisses her, she again feels she is losing him. They walk past the warren of unroofed, low walls, where the wealthy of ancient Rome once constructed their lavish palaces and ornate temples, to the steps that descend to the Forum, the same ruins Raffaello spent his final years cataloguing.

" 'Nearly all people regard him as a God sent from Heaven to restore to the Eternal City its ancient majesty,' " Tulia quotes from her reading. A lone pink foxglove grows between two fallen stones, and she reaches down to stroke its velvety petals. It is starting to wilt, so she pours some water from her bottle over the dusty soil. "How do you think Raffaello really died?" she asks. "There are as many theories on his death as there are on his love life. It's hard to know what to believe."

They pass a pockmarked arch. "On the contrary, it is very simple," Raphael says. "He perished from a fever, caught in one of the damp excavation sites. He suffered for days in a delirium. Not even the pope's own physician could help him. When it came time for him to breathe his last, Pope Leo himself gave him the last rites. And then he returned to God, who welcomed him back to heaven. It was his birthday, Good Friday, the same day Christ died."

"He was so young," she says quietly.

"You are unhappy, *cara*."

"It saddens me to think of him dying. I feel as though I've come to know him."

"Do not be sad. It all happened a very long time ago. And there is nothing mere mortals can do to change the past." They are outside the Forum now, back in the frenzied streets. A man holds out a bundle of long-stemmed roses, and Raphael buys one with a crumpled bill he pulls from his vest pocket.

"To cheer you up," he says as he hands her the flower. "You are a *Rosa,* after all." She thanks him but can't help remembering a time when he might have produced the rose by magic.

That summer died

*I*t is in her eyes, he thought. Confusion. It was there again after they made love, and he wondered, not for the first time, how long he could keep his vow. Or if it was even right to do so.

Outside the wind whistled through loose roof tiles and ripped a shutter from its hinges. He knew that in the garden, snow swirled through the dark, drifting against the stone walls, clinging to the bare rose vines, blanketing the blackened mint and withered poppy stems. But inside her little cottage with the shutters firmly closed, the fire crackling, and the doors covered with tapestries that he had brought from his own apartments to keep out the drafts, it was warm. The tapestries, the little desk where she now sat writing, the warm cape that hung beside the bed—these were among the few gifts she had allowed him to make. It is enough that I rely on you to live and work, she had said, and he feared sometimes her pride would be her undoing.

In front of him on the old wooden table lay a list of measurements and the detailed sketches he had made of an imperial palace on Palatine Hill. But he could not concentrate tonight on Rome's lost glories, only on the glory that was this woman seated at the writing desk she had pulled close to the fire. With her head bent over her work, the jewels in her golden comb were in themselves little fires. She wrote slowly, forming her letters with care, pausing between each word or phrase to stare into the flames as if there she could see her next line. She never edited what she wrote, standing by every word she committed to paper.

She adjusted the candle, pulling it closer to the page. The fire snapped, and a burst of sparks hovered for a moment over the hearth before burning out. Fireflies, he thought. There were fireflies at the villa outside Firenze. Little pinpoints of pure light in the velvety darkness. The two of them had lain in the grass, hands clasped. It is as if we are floating among the stars, she had said.

He had made his vow at the villa. Never to utter those words. The words he knew she wanted to hear. He could not even find in his heart the strength to tell her why. My destiny is in the hands of His Holiness, he thought, although he imagined His Holiness would take it even further. Not in my hands, he would say, but in God's. Either way, his fate was not his own. And so he had made this silent vow to spare her, but more and more he believed it to be futile. She wanted to hear those words and he wanted to say them. If he could not stay with her, would they give her the strength to move on—to be happy, knowing that for him to leave her would never be his choice? Or could mere words ever be enough, given that her work and very life depended upon him?

He was hardly aware he had picked up his quill again. He dipped it into his pot of ink and on a fresh page drew an arc, heavy at first before trailing off into nothingness. It was a line she had forbidden him to make, but he dipped his pen into the pot again and a second arc followed the first. Outside, the wind battered the little house.

He had gone to Chigi's villa earlier that day, standing next to the fresco he had painted for his friend. Galatea, the most desirable woman who ever lived, he thought, until he met his beloved. He had gone with the intention of asking his friend's advice. There is this woman, he meant to say, for he would not mention her name. What would you do, my friend? But

Chigi, as if he already knew what Raffaello wanted, reminded him of the great privilege he enjoyed as a member of the papal court. Enjoyed by so few artists. You were called to serve His Holiness by God himself, Chigi had said. They had walked around the grounds just as the first flakes began to fall, and when Raffaello declined his invitation to dine, Chigi had offered him a brace of pheasants.

He had returned to the Vatican and presented the birds to the kitchens. I only desire one for myself, he told the ruddy-faced cook. It was returned to him a few hours later, bereft of its feathers, stuffed with bread and nuts and raisins, roasted to the color of honey. The cook, whose face was redder than ever, waved away the coins he offered him. He thanked him and went to send his students home for the night. It was still early and the work was far behind schedule, but the snow was getting heavier and the wind stronger. Besides, he was anxious to get away to her cottage.

He looked now from his beloved's face back to the paper where her features were taking shape. I would paint her just as she is now, he thought, more lovely than the Madonna herself. This ideal he had always sought— and was now feeling powerless to hold and protect. And what if something should ever happen to him? Who would look after her then?

At that moment, a gust of wind struck the cottage and rattled the cups on the shelves. It startled him, as it did the cat curled up on the bed. The cat jumped down and brushed against the legs of his mistress as if to reassure her of his watchful presence before going over to the plate under the shelves and sampling a little more of the pheasant they had left him. "Is it wise for you to keep this animal?" Raffaello had asked her once. "You will be taken for a witch one day." She dismissed his caution with a wave of her hand, asking how it was that in a city crawling with rats it was cats people feared. He said something about superstitions not being rational, and before kissing him, she replied that he worried too much.

Perhaps it was true, he thought. Only in her arms did he feel this dread leave him. There he forgot everything, as he had a few hours before when he had arrived at her door just as the light was dying, pheasant wrapped in a towel from the papal kitchens. He had sent his servant away at her gate, wishing him haste as he took from him the jugs of wine and water and the bundle of wood for the fire.

Inside he had set down his packages, hung up his snowy cloak, and, with barely a greeting, led her to bed. There he tried to show what he could not say with his kisses. It was little wonder confusion shadowed her eyes.

He made another line across the page. Wide and soft like a brushstroke. And another, the curve of a lash against a cheek.

When he looked up, she was standing over him. Was that sadness in her eyes now, or disappointment? "What are you doing?" she asked quietly. "It is my likeness." He could barely hear her voice over the wind.

"You looked so beautiful, I could not help myself." If he couldn't tell her he loved her with words, then let him do it like this.

She picked up the sheet, and a fresh trail of ink flowed down the paper. She held it for a moment, opened her mouth as if to say something, then closed it again before taking the drawing and wordlessly placing it on the fire. When she turned back to him, it was with tears in her eyes. He knew then that it was more than just words he owed her. If he did not find a way to live with her openly and honestly, he would lose her. But they were at an impasse: she would not be known as his mistress, and he could not make her his wife. They stared at each other until she returned to her desk and he to his measurements.

The last time

Tulia watches Raphael sleep. Miss Mercy, who, she is sure, has waxed poetic for pages about Keats and Shelley in Rome, sits unopened on her bedside table. She will press the rose Raphael gave her between its pages alongside the torn plane ticket and the prayer card from the Chiesa dell'Angelo Raffaele. Raphael lies on his back, his olive complexion darkened by the brilliant sunshine of the last few weeks. Her very own artist. Her Raffaello made real. His chest rises and falls, and one hand, bearing no trace of chalk, rests on his stomach. The other arm is stretched over her pillow. She has no idea of course what the Renaissance master was really like, but for her these men have become one and the same. She rests her head on his shoulder and feels him pull her closer as she drifts into a familiar dream. Only this time, there's no mist. Everything is clear.

She is herself. Alone, in the tiny cottage of the woman in her book. The woman with the oranges. The artist's beloved. She is she. She is crying, sobbing. She gets up from her desk, leaving her quill and ink bottle and paper scattered on the surface, and goes into the garden, still half asleep from winter. It is cold and drizzling, but she does not wear a shawl and does not care. Only a few buds grace the skeletons of trees. Only a few green shoots are visible in the brown earth.

Raffaello is dead. Raffaello. Painter. Painter of angels. Her angel. Her Raffaello.

She has just found out at the market, the day before Easter. When he did not return that night, she went to his studio, only to be turned away by a servant. "He is ill," the servant said. Not knowing the illness to be so serious, she did not press the point or leave her name. How she wished she had. Roma may be in mourning, but she is devastated.

She rips the golden comb out of her hair, throws it to the ground, watches it sink, the brown mud closing over the red stones. The only relic she has from her mother, gone. She knows there will be no more beauty in her life. She will never see him again. Never tell him how much she loves him. Never hear him say the same thing. She runs her hands along the crumbling stone walls. Roman ruins, he told her the first day they met, the day he read her writing and decided he would be her patron, the day their love was born. She will never write again . . .

A knock on the door interrupts her thoughts, and she is illogically hopeful. She reenters the cottage, drying her eyes. But only a neighbor stands there, urging her to follow, and she does so, blindly. "Did you hear?" the old woman asks as they head to the main street. She is clearly enjoying the excitement. "The loggia at the Vatican fell on Good Friday. They are saying it is a miracle, a sign that foretold the moment of the maestro's death." And the old woman crosses herself several times.

Hundreds have gathered to see the last procession of His Holiness's favorite artist—the prince of painters—before his funeral mass at the Vatican and burial in the Pantheon. She pushes her way through the weeping crowd to the pallet being carried by Swiss Guards and looks right at his face.

It is Raphael.

"Shhh, Tulia, everything is okay." Raphael is holding her, while from outside their hotel room rises the plaintive wail of sirens. She

clutches his arms and studies him in the bluish glow of the street-
lights, not knowing for a moment what is dream, what is reality.
Then she realizes that Raphael really is here, breath and flesh and
blood. "Your dream is back," he says in a soothing tone. "You were
talking in your sleep."

"Yes," she says. "I . . . I . . . was dreaming about what you told
me earlier. About Raffaello's death." She leans back on the pillow,
her breath more steady now. "I've spent so much time on my book,
I think I'm dreaming myself into it. It seemed so real." She hesitates, not wanting to tell him all the details. That she dreamed *she*
was Raffaello's beloved. And that it was Raphael—not Raffaello—
who died in her dreams. "So real I thought my own heart would
break," she says.

"You have been working hard, *cara*."

"I guess you could say that I've come to love Raffaello through
my writing. I can't bear the thought of his death." She turns to face
him. "Maybe it's because when I write about Raffaello, it's you I
picture." She feels again what it would be like to lose him, to never
again have the chance to tell him how deeply she cares about him.
She can't take that chance. "I love you," she says, looking straight
into his eyes. Brimming instantly with tears, they reflect back
what she feels. *And you love me. Please tell me you love me too.*

But he doesn't say it, only pulls her close and makes love to her
for what seems like forever. She tries to remember every look,
every kiss, wondering all the while if this is the last time.

We said good-bye

Raffaello kissed her good-bye at the door and stepped out into the driving rain. He turned, and she was still there, leaning against the door frame, the blanket from the bed draped over her thin nightdress like a cape. Her hair tumbled around her shoulders, framing her exquisite face. Her eyes were so soft, so full of love, it was all he could do not to run back into her arms. How he would love to spend the day at her side, listening to the sound of rain on the roof, a warm fire warding off the early-spring chill.

Only the thought that he would be back that night gave him the strength to turn away. He walked through the streets almost oblivious to his surroundings and the rain that streamed down from lead-gray skies. *I love you*, he whispered over and over, rehearsing the words he would finally say out loud that night for the very first time.

He hurried along the banks of the swollen Tevere River to a large stately house, where he was expected for a business appointment. In the man's study, he finalized the deal he had been planning for weeks. A fire roared in the large fireplace, but the papers were signed so quickly his clothes did not have a chance to dry. He did not care. He left the house in the direction of the ruins, having bought the future site of a villa. Their villa. His wedding gift to her—though he had yet to ask her if she would marry him.

He did not want to keep their relationship a secret any longer. For almost a year he had loved her, spending every moment he could at her cottage or at his friend's villa in the hills above Firenze. And while she refused to be known as his mistress, he prayed she would be happy to be known as his wife. He did not care that she had no dowry, no connections. He no longer cared what the papal court thought. He would plead his case before His Holiness and accept whatever the consequences were. His mind was made up. He was marrying her not for money or lineage or status but for love. He wanted to wake up every morning and see her there beside him. He wanted her voice to be the last thing he heard before falling asleep. He wanted her to be the mother of his children.

And he wanted to paint her at last. For if she could be known to history as his wife, she would no longer have a reason to refuse. He wanted so desperately to capture her beauty, her smile, the way she looked at him, the way she loved him and he her. He wanted to show this all in her portrait. How many times had he painted the Madonna? In every painting he had tried to capture what he thought was his ideal of beauty, but not one came close to this woman he loved. He whispered her name again as he entered the pits where the excavations were taking place.

The rain did not let up, and he slogged among the ancient stones, taking measurements that he committed to memory, as it was too wet for ink and paper. In his mind he saw these slabs not as ruins, not as broken columns scattered in the mud, but as they once must have looked in all their magnificence, rising toward the sun, a tribute to some great god. He could not bear them to be lost to history, for each one had a story to tell. He stepped into a deep hole, his boot filling with water. Rain flowed from his hair into his eyes. Realizing he was making little headway, he gave up at midday and walked to his studio to check the progress of his students.

He had not been very good at fulfilling his commitments this past year.

Patrons were clamoring for work to be finished, and his students were stretched to their limits. He knew that rumors about him abounded. Even his dear friend Chigi had asked what kept him from the work he loved. But he had fulfilled his promise to her, and no one knew of her existence. That would change after they married. He hated keeping his love secret when he wanted to shout it from the city walls.

The studio was in an uproar when he arrived, and he was immediately surrounded by young men, all appealing to him to take their side in some dispute. Guiltily, he realized that if his students were not always up for the challenges he set out for them, it was largely his fault. He vowed that also would change. He would take on less work and concentrate only on what truly excited him. He was a rich man. He need not do everything. And it would give him more time with his beloved.

Suddenly, the studio felt sweltering1y hot. The smell of paint overwhelmed him. He felt weak and tired. What was wrong? He had felt better than fine only this morning. His drenched cloak weighed him down, but he no longer had the strength to remove it. He looked at the animated faces around him and felt he would suffocate if they did not move back. But he did not have the vigor to tell them.

"What is it, maestro?" This voice as if from far away was the last thing he heard before he dropped to the floor, his limbs too weak to support him.

When he woke up, only his student Giulio Romano sat beside him. He was lying on the narrow bed in the studio, a place he had often slept when he had worked into the night. But not lately, not when he could steal through the streets and be in her arms.

"My God," he tried to cry out. "What time is it? I must return to her!" But he did not know if the words escaped his lips or not. Giulio pressed a cool cloth against the heat of his forehead. He tried to raise his arm to push it away, but it lay lifeless as a stone at his side.

"You have been unconscious for more than two days," Giulio said soothingly. "You have been burning with fever. I have told the others to go, for fear of the plague, but I see no signs of it. Only this terrible fever."

Giulio removed the warmed rag from his forehead and dipped it into a pan of cold water, wringing it out and applying it again. "His Holiness came this morning and read you the last rites. The doctor said he hoped there would be no need, but His Holiness knew that if you took a turn for the worse, you would not want to die without the rites."

The man's words swirled around his mind. Plague. Last rites. Two days—he had been unconscious for two days. He closed his eyes and saw her standing in the doorway, draped in the blanket from the bed, those eyes so full of love. She would have waited for him. He had failed her. He tried to speak, but while he could make his lips move, no sound came out.

Giulio let water drip from a spoon onto his parched lips. "Do not try to speak, maestro. Just rest. Save your strength."

Raffaello could do nothing but heed Giulio's advice as darkness swallowed him again. But the darkness was not complete, for he kept seeing her there. And himself, standing in the rain, repeating, I love you, but not saying it aloud. He knew he was dying, and while he did not fear death, he raged against heaven and then himself for the timing. Why now? And why had he waited? Why had he not just said it? He knew he was mortal, he knew that death could come at any time. And now she would never know how much he loved her. Enough to make her his wife. More than his own life.

When consciousness returned, he saw Pope Leo standing over his bed. He read the concern in His Holiness's face, and he knew the time was near. If only he could tell him to find her, to say that he loved her, to be sure that she would be taken care of after his death. What would become of her now? Oh God, why now?

"Do not struggle, Raffaello," His Holiness said. "You will be missed on earth, but in heaven you will be received by angels."

And Raffaello already saw them, waiting for him. They stood behind His Holiness in a bright pool of light. Like the angels he had spent his life painting, with white wings, ready to receive him into their embrace. Waiting for him. He tried to call to them, to reason. Please. I am not ready. Just *a bit longer. Let me paint her. Just let me tell her . . . But even as he pleaded, he knew they had no power to grant him more life. They were only the messengers. At least he could sense sympathy in their beatific eyes.*

"It is time to go home now, Raffaello," His Holiness said gently, tears running down his cheeks. Raffaello heard the murmured last rites said again for him. And now there was nothing left to do but close his eyes and pray, not for himself but for the woman waiting for him. He prayed she would forgive him. He prayed she would be strong and find safety and happiness on her own. But most of all, he prayed she would know he loved her and would through all eternity.

"It is time to go home." And it was time. I wept as I remembered . . . Very slowly he reached out and took the hand that was sent to guide him. Away from her. His very own angel.

And with his last breath, afloat in the night, her name like a prayer.

And tears fall

Clouds thicken overhead, and the sun struggles to reveal itself as Tulia passes the obelisk in front of the Pantheon. By the time she is inside and looks up through the oculus in the dome's center, she can see only gray sky. She almost hadn't come, as Raphael had refused to accompany her. "It is too gray a day to be looking at graves," he said. "But you go. It is important. I will wait for you in the park."

At the villa she was content to live for the moment, to not worry about the future. But it was easier then, when time stood still and she thought it would last forever. Now her plane leaves from Heathrow tomorrow afternoon, and her time remaining with Raphael can be counted in hours. Yet they have not discussed their future together, and she is terrified he won't ask her to stay. Had she not met him, she would be in England right now, probably ready to return home and resume her life in New York. Now she never wants to go back.

She slowly walks along the edge of the curved marble walls past the tomb of Vittorio Emanuele to the object of her visit, the elaborate sarcophagus of the artist Raffaello Sanzio. Above the tomb is *Madonna del Sasso,* the Madonna of the Rock, her foot resting on a boulder, the Christ child cradled in her arms.

On the tomb, Tulia lays the red poppies she bought from a vendor. "From your beloved," she whispers. She is certain that while she still lived, she must have come here often. To say a prayer. To leave a flower. Tulia hopes she is paying him proper tribute in her novel.

She runs her fingers over the cool stone, tracing the Latin letters, knowing already what they translate to in English: *This is Raffaello's tomb—While he lived, Nature feared he'd overshadow her, and when he died, Nature feared she too would die.*

Next to Raffaello's tomb is the grave of Maria Bibbiena, a woman he was supposed to marry, but who died so young, a woman who wasn't his true love, whom he may have never even met.

I am myself well, but I feel as if I was no more in Roma now that my poor Raffaello is gone. Castiglione wrote that upon Raffaello's death. And if Castiglione, a friend, felt that way, Tulia can only imagine the agony his beloved must have experienced from losing him, from never hearing him say he loved her. Never realizing the life he was planning for them. Not knowing what would come next for her as she faced the world alone. Even sacrificing her writing, for she had lost her muse.

What would have happened to her? No one other than a handful of servants knew she even existed. In the best-case scenario, if her uncle still helped, maybe she found more work as a translator or perhaps even as a companion or maid. But could her uncle have supported her with his own family to consider? Not likely.

What about a convent then, the choice of many other single women at the time? That would have afforded her both security and a certain measure of independence. But Tulia is sure she would not have entered a nunnery. Even if she had the means, she did not have the requisite belief.

Might she have become a courtesan or a common prostitute? Tulia doubts this as well. She had enormous pride and little ability to compromise her beliefs. She wanted to be independent at a time when women couldn't be. And as she wrote in her first letter to Raffaello, she would rather die.

Would she have taken her own life then? Was that the only alternative? Or did she put a sharp blade to her throat and find herself unable to make the slice?

Could she have survived the 1527 sacking of Rome, when the papal treasures were pillaged, the Sistine Chapel was used as a barn, and women were reportedly raped on the altars? Or did her radical ideas bring her to harm as Raffaello feared? And what about the epidemics of plague and other pestilence that frequently swept the city? Or any of the other countless calamities that a woman alone in so brutal a world may have encountered?

What became of her manuscripts? Her volume of Petrarch? Raffaello's letters? Did she hide them under some loose plank in the floor of her cottage? Or did she burn them to keep warm on a particularly bitter night?

No matter what fate had in store for her, though, would she have been able to forgive Raffaello? She probably felt abandoned by him, yet the relationship was largely on her terms. He wanted to paint her, to make her existence known, but she refused. He wanted to publish her writing right away; she declined that too. In the end, might she have regretted these decisions?

How would her life have been different if her portrait had been painted and her writings published? If Raffaello's friends and associates knew of her? Would she have been able to enter their circle and find another patron? Or would they have forgotten about her?

Tulia can't bear writing any of this down, all the grim possibilities too bleak to bear. Better to leave the rest of the beloved's story lost to history.

She herself is having trouble forgiving Raffaello. True, his beloved had been stubborn. And he was so young when he died—only thirty-seven. And while he was making provisions for them just before his death, he should have mentioned her in a will. He knew she would be in jeopardy without him. With his wealth, she could have continued writing and been taken care of for the rest of her life.

Most of all, how could Raffaello never have told his beloved he loved her?

And why doesn't the sidewalk artist tell her he loves her? Can she forgive him if he leaves her? She knows Raphael loves her, she's known since the first time they made love. But why is he holding back from telling her what he so clearly feels?

If he only knew how she longed to hear those words from him. Just like Raffaello's beloved. So simple. *I love you.* They would give her the strength to move on alone if she must. Maybe he is hoping to spare her feelings, so that it will be easier if the time comes for them to say good-bye.

She prays, though, that it doesn't come to that. She prays instead that she and Raphael will live together to a ripe old age, painting and writing and loving each other.

Great Archangel Raffaele, please hear my prayer . . .

The gray has partially dissolved and hazy rays stream through the oculus, casting shimmering prisms along the walls, light dancing with shadow. The sunbeams cross her shoulders like the memory of a lover's embrace.

On the wings of angels

By the time Tulia reaches the gardens by the Villa Borghese, it is almost dark and she can smell the spring rain imminent on the wind. Far ahead, Raphael is crouched at the edge of the street, a cigarette held between his chalk-smudged fingers as he scrutinizes the sidewalk. She hurries over to him, and he rises to kiss her.

"More sidewalk art," she says as she leans down to inspect his work. She is shocked to see her own likeness staring back. Blue eyes full of emotion. Brown hair in loose tangles over one bare shoulder. A sheer white shawl draped over the other arm. Poppies dotting the green grass. The azure sky above.

"Do you like it?" he asks.

She looks up at him exhaling sweet smoke, dressed in his familiar vest and jeans worn at the knees, his dark hair tucked behind his ears. *He is so beautiful.* Then she looks back to the painting. "It's amazing."

He seems relieved. "I am glad you think so."

"Is this a copy of the painting you made of me at the villa? I wish you would let me see the original."

"I hope one day."

"I don't know how you can stand it—all this work, knowing it won't be here tomorrow." As if to emphasize her point, the rain begins to punctuate the concrete. The poppies start to smear, and raindrops dot her cheeks like tears.

He shrugs as he stubs out his cigarette and starts to gather his supplies. "This is my story for now, I suppose."

But what about their story? She tries to quell her rising panic by helping to stack his boxes of chalk, her words tumbling over one another. "I really wish I could see your other paintings, the ones you create to last. In fact, I wish you would show them to the world. Display them in a gallery somewhere."

He doesn't answer, intent on neatly packing his weatherworn bag. After putting away the last box, he asks, "It is not my paintings you are worried about, is it, *cara?*" He pulls an umbrella out of his bag's side pocket, and it blooms above them as they begin to walk through the early-evening drizzle.

They head toward the river. He takes her hands in his and runs his rough fingers across her smooth palms. His touch is as gentle as an angel's, as sure as an artist's.

This is the moment, right? He will ask her now to stay with him in Europe. *Raffaele, please hear my prayer . . .*

"There are no happily-ever-afters, you know that," he says solemnly. "But there will be other stories, wonderful stories that have yet to begin. Promise me you will concentrate on them."

Her insides crumple. This is the moment she has feared. She doesn't want a new story. She wants Raphael.

"I know," he whispers, and he stops to face her. "I do not want this either." He looks at her, his eyes shining, and she can read the love in them. "I vow to you, I wish I could. I have tried everything I can think of. If I could, I would move heaven and earth. God knows how much I have prayed. But it is impossible."

They are standing on the Sant'Angelo Bridge. The air is fragrant with rain, and Bellini's marble angels stand with outstretched wings, haloed in mist under the lights of the bridge. St. Peter's Basilica rises in the distance.

"Why? *Why* can't you? I would do anything to be with you." This is happening too fast, she thinks. Give me more time with him. *Please . . .*

He looks distraught. "I do not blame you for being angry."

Not knowing what to say, she pulls her hands from his and steps out of the shelter of the umbrella to the stone rail. She doesn't want him to see her cry. She stares at St. Peter's, then looks up at the embracing angel wings and feels the rain start to mingle with her tears. Rain, which always fills her with a sense of loss. Why rain now, when she has to say good-bye? Why does she have to say good-bye anyway?

Behind her, he doesn't move, though she can hear his ragged breathing. Her own breath comes out heavy and irregular too. Then she hears him take a step and the umbrella covers her again. She feels his arm around her, drawing her to him. She relents, leaning against his chest, his breath warm on the top of her head, and wonders if her portrait by the Villa Borghese is completely washed away by now. She won't even have that to remember him by.

She slowly turns around to look up at him, and he smiles sadly. "I guess I should say good-bye then," she says with more strength than she feels.

His eyes are filled with tears. "I hope you will be able to forgive me, Tulia," he says. "I do not know exactly when, but I promise one day you will understand." He caresses her face as if trying to memorize every nuance. "Even though you will not be able to see me, I will always be with you. You just have to close your eyes and dream."

"I know how to do that," she says.

He passes her the umbrella. "I need you to believe this is not what I want. Do you love me enough to believe that?"

She trembles again, not from any anger this time but from the intensity of emotion, the purity of his love pouring into her. "Yes." Whatever his reasons, she can see his torment. She can't comprehend it, but she will have to accept it. "I wonder if I'll ever know your real name."

"I like Raphael."

"I love you, Raphael." She says it, not expecting any response.

He smiles then, freely and with pure joy. "I love you too, Tulia. I always have."

She closes her eyes as he kisses her. She smells springtime blossoms. Hears the river meandering under their feet. Rain splattering on the fabric of the umbrella. The air is muggy and warm.

When she opens her eyes, she sees the wings of Bellini's angels above her. The clouds part, and a sliver of moon touches the wings with gold.

Raphael. Painter. Painter of angels. Her angel.

Her Raphael is gone.

I'll never forget

Thanks for meeting me," Ethan says, kissing Tulia lightly on the cheek before resuming his seat at the bar. They are at a bistro on the Upper West Side. It is early and the bar is almost empty, but a pianist is already playing jazz standards at a baby grand. Outside, the October wind hints at winter.

"It's good to see you, Ethan." Tulia takes off her coat and lays it across a stool. Ethan looks as handsome as she remembers him, fit and trim in his charcoal-gray Italian suit. She has not seen him in over a year and a half, not since the day she left for Europe, and she does not know if it feels like just yesterday or a lifetime ago. "How's Jasmine?"

"All right, I guess," he says, swirling the olive around his almost-empty martini glass. His cell phone sits on the bar in front of him. "Haven't seen her in a while."

"Oh, I'm sorry," Tulia says. "I didn't realize."

"No problem. It was pretty sudden, I guess. She decided that things weren't working out. You know how it goes."

Tulia can almost hear Jasmine's voice. *The minute I find myself picking up someone else's socks, I'm out of there.* And while Tulia knows that Jasmine was speaking figuratively, she can almost see the offending socks lying in a crumpled heap by his side of the bed.

"You should call her sometime. I'm sure she'd love to hear from you." He puts down his empty glass. "I know she feels badly about what happened."

Tulia can't help but think the feeling badly part didn't come until the magic started wearing off with Ethan. On her return from Europe, she went to the apartment while Ethan was at work to pick up her things. In the closet, her clothes and shoes were jumbled together with Jasmine's. After sorting through them, she left a brief note, wishing them both well, but Jasmine never responded, and Tulia knew the friendship was over. If it ever was one.

Ethan signals the bartender, and Tulia orders a Chianti and he another martini. She always drinks Chianti now—memories of making love in the garden of a Tuscan villa, the sun shining through the leaves, poppies swaying on delicate stems . . .

"What about the guy you met in Europe? Was it just a vacation romance, or are you still seeing him?"

How can she tell him she sees him everywhere? She has only just now come from the Metropolitan Museum of Art. She's been there many times since her return to see their Raffaello Madonna. She can sense the presence of her own Raphael there, and it is all she can do not to lay her cheek against the paint.

She can sense her Raphael, too, in the few sidewalk artists she has seen on the Manhattan streets. She never fails to throw a couple of dollars into their hats, the very act conjuring up the image of a pair of pensive chalk angels, a bouquet being drawn from a sleeve . . .

She looks at Ethan and can see a bit of hope, and she knows he is interested in her answer. "Just a vacation romance." It is perhaps not the best response. She can tell Ethan is lonely now and looking to her to fill a gap in his life, but she doesn't know what else to say.

"How unfortunate for him." He seems pleased. "You look wonderful, you know. And that dress looks great on you."

"Thanks, Ethan." She doesn't tell him it is an old dress that he never liked before. He fails to notice her shoes, the ones she was wearing the day she met Raphael.

He sips his martini. "I read in a magazine article that you bought a house in the Poconos. You always wanted a place there."

She nods. "It's on the same lake where my family had their cabin. I spend as much time as I can there." That first month back, she immersed herself in the details of regular life. Moving out of Ethan's, talking to her publisher, negotiating an advance, buying the house with it. She was relieved when her editor agreed to take *For My Beloved* on the basis of only a few chapters, and she promised them a finished manuscript by Thanksgiving. All summer and fall was spent in the new house, losing herself in the book, writing into every line her own happiness, her own loss. Lulled to sleep by the lap of waves against the shore. Finding comfort in the rumble of a summer storm and the soft sound of rain.

"I read your book too," Ethan is saying. "I hear it's doing well. I'm not surprised. It's very good. Sad, but good."

"Thanks. I'm very happy with how it's doing." She wonders again, as she so often does, if Raphael has read it too. If he is bragging to people that he knew her, as he said he would.

"Can I ask you a question though?" Ethan asks. "Why do you never tell us the woman's name—the beloved? I kept expecting to find out who she was."

"I get this question a lot. It's because nobody knows who she was. Except Raffaello, that is. She's lost to history. I thought the best way of showing that was not to give her a name."

"Can you be sure she existed then?"

There is no point in trying to explain—how she has come to believe this woman really did exist. "No," she says. "But it's a good story."

"I wasn't being critical," Ethan adds hastily. "It was a great book."

"Don't apologize. It's a valid question."

He stares into his drink. "I have to confess that I never finished your first book."

She laughs. It doesn't hurt, this admission on his part, and she knows she is truly free of him. "I always suspected as much, even though the book feels as much yours as mine. Do you even remember the name of it?"

He looks at her, embarrassed. "Sorry," he says, and she feels he means it.

"It's okay. You really didn't miss much. By the way, I heard you made managing director. Congratulations. I know how much you wanted it."

"Thanks," he says, and she is surprised to see that he looks slightly disappointed. Perhaps this promotion isn't the holy grail he hoped for.

His cell phone rings, and he excuses himself to answer it, getting up from the bar and going to stand by the window.

It is strange being here with Ethan. More so because she'd rather be meeting Raphael. The pianist pauses before starting a new song. "Ne Me Quitte Pas." Don't Leave Me.

Why couldn't they be together? She asks herself this often, but nothing makes sense. She wants to believe he loved her absolutely and completely, that he wanted to be with her as much as she wanted to be with him. But perhaps in the end he couldn't forget her after all—the woman with the oranges. Tulia was always aware of something weighing on him—something she could not help him forget. Are they together again? Married? Happy? Or are they still apart and is he, for all his words about not hanging on to old stories, still unable to let go?

I will always be with you. You just have to close your eyes and dream. And while she does meet him in her dreams—not the dream that used to instill such despair, but new, sweet ones to which she always looks forward—what she wouldn't give to open her eyes and see him standing there.

Those first few months she almost believed he would find her in New York or the mountains, as he had found her in Venice and Florence. A knock on the door, the glimpse of a dark ponytail in a crowd—these small things would fill her with momentary hope, only to have that hope dashed when the person at the door was a neighbor, the man on the street a stranger. And as the days became weeks and then months, she knew it was not going to happen. Their story was over.

I promise one day you will understand.

I am trying, Raphael.

I love you. She hears his voice in the sound of the rain. *I always have . . .* The only thing that makes this separation bearable.

"Earth to Tulia." She looks up at Ethan standing next to her. He touches her shoulder briefly before resuming his seat. "Sorry about that. Panicky client." He takes a sip of his martini. "What were you so deep in thought about?"

"Nothing," she says, her voice a little shaky.

He looks at her closely, and she can tell he is summoning his courage. "Can I take you out for dinner tonight?" he asks, a little shyly and without his usual assurance.

He looks hopeful, but Tulia shakes her head. "Thanks. But I don't think it's such a good idea."

He lowers his voice. "We used to be so good together, Tulia. Do you remember that first night when we rode the Staten Island ferry? The city was ours back then."

It used to be her reminding him of such things.

Over time, our lovers become stories we can go back to and remember how they were written.

"I remember," she says gently. "But it's time to move on. I'm sure you'll meet someone wonderful."

There is more than one happy ending.

But as she often wonders how well Raphael followed his own advice, she now considers how well she can follow her own. Because since Raphael left her in Rome, it is almost impossible to believe she can ever be that happy again.

Love

W hat's the matter, Mildred?" Tulia asks, pushing her chair back from her desk and scooping up the cat she has named after Miss Mercy. "Are you feeling neglected?" Worried meows give way to contented purrs.

Mildred has been her constant companion since the stormy June night when Tulia found her wet and shaking outside her door. The cat did not belong to any of the houses around the lake, and there was consensus among her neighbors that it had been dropped from a car and abandoned, a practice that happened only too often.

Tulia strokes the cat on her lap as she prints off her afternoon's work. She closes the volume of Petrarch sonnets and the book on Italian life in the Middle Ages and stacks them next to her copy of Miss Mercy. She doesn't open Miss Mercy to look at the rose pressed between the pages. She does that less often these days. The Petrarch volume, the rose, the plane ticket, and the prayer card are the only physical reminders that Raphael was real. She wishes sometimes she had photographs, but she never even packed her camera.

Taking the pages from the printer, she places them in a folder beside her computer. While her new novel on Petrarch and Laura is going well, she fears it is not as inspired as *For My Beloved* was. Not surprising, as there is no sidewalk artist or poet named Petrarch to act as her muse. Her next book, she vows, will be set here, in the lakes and mountains that surround her home. She knows she can't keep hanging on to Raphael through her writing.

The screen door slams and her mother comes in, her reading glasses on a chain around her neck and a thick book tucked under her arm. Tulia looks out the windows facing the lake and through the trees sees her father still seated in the deck chair at the end of the dock. "Go keep your father company, dear," her mother says. "I'm going to start the rabbit." At the word "rabbit," Mildred jumps down from Tulia's lap and goes to rub against her mother's legs.

Tulia's mother has taken up cooking in her retirement, all in the name of research. She has become intrigued by the diet of the Anglo-Saxons and tries to reproduce dishes that may have been eaten at the time of Beowulf. And while Tulia cringes at the quantities of meat her parents have consumed in recent months, Mildred couldn't be happier.

Buttoning her cardigan, Tulia goes out to join her father. Although she has visited her parents in Pittsburgh several times since her return, this is the first time they have visited her, the occasion being her mother's birthday. They balked at the long drive, but she convinced them to take the train, picking them up from the station in Philadelphia. Impractical as ever, they arrived lugging suitcases overflowing with books, newspapers, and magazines, including recent *Times Literary Supplement*s and several back issues of the *London Review of Books*. Although they are both finally retired from teaching, they still write articles for various journals, and her father has brought his briefcase stuffed with notes for his latest paper, while her mother dragged a gargantuan cooler filled with the ingredients for her cooking experiments. Only a smaller piece of luggage holds any clothes at all, and they both have forgotten their toothbrushes. Within minutes of their arrival, they planted themselves in the wingback chairs on either side of the fireplace and sent Tulia in search of stronger lightbulbs for reading.

She finds her father now gazing out across the water, his book seemingly forgotten, facedown on his lap. She is struck by how old he looks; his face has developed soft jowls, and his unkempt white hair has become thin and wispy. "You can see the old place from here," he says as Tulia takes the chair beside him. And it is true, they can just make it out across the lake, dwarfed by the tall pines. The mountains that ring the lake swell softly from the earth, hallmark of the low-slung Appalachian chain. It is the weekend after Labor Day, and most of the residents have left for the season. Already a few trees are tinged with orange. "Do you still have your apartment in New York?" her father asks, eyes still fixed on the opposite shore.

She nods, "I sublet it for the summer. I'd like to stay here until Thanksgiving. I bought lots of firewood, and there's a propane heater if it gets really cold." She has promised Mr. Sims that she will be back in time to work at the bookstore for the holiday season. Also Tom (or is it Tod?) is getting married on New Year's Eve, and she is looking forward to the wedding.

"Ever see that Ethan fellow?" A second question. From her father two questions constitute a flood, and she wonders what has brought this on.

"Once. Last fall."

"Can't say your mother and I were too upset when you broke it off. He wasn't right for you. Not a poetic bone in his body." Her mother once went so far as to say "He seems nice, dear," but this is the first time her father has ever expressed an opinion on the matter. They only met him a few times. Once in New York when they came to the city for a symposium, the other times over the holidays when Tulia and Ethan would make the dutiful appearance on

Christmas Eve before flying to Connecticut to spend Christmas Day with Ethan's parents and sister.

"Why didn't you say anything at the time if you didn't like him?"

"Didn't think it would do much good. Your mother's parents were more than adamant that we not marry. I think it made us more determined than ever. That's why we eloped."

"Eloped? You and Mom eloped? I didn't know that. Why were they so set against you?"

"They didn't think I was good enough for their daughter. They were from Boston, and the blood in their veins was bluer than this lake. They didn't like their daughter going to graduate school either. Filled her head with atheist ideas, they said. And it interfered with their mission of marrying her off to another Boston Brahmin type—I think they had a Kennedy in mind. They pretty much disowned her after we were married, and that was without them knowing I was only second-generation American. They could trace their own lineage back to the *Mayflower*. My father's insistence on anglicizing the family name paid off, I guess. They assumed Rose was a good solid English name. Have I not told you this before?"

Tulia shakes her head. She doesn't know any of this. Outside of discussions about literature, this might also be one of the longest conversations she's ever had with her father. They look up as a flock of Canada geese fly over on their way south. Flying one behind the other, they form a neat *V*, and the quiet afternoon is filled with their distinctive honking.

"Ironically," her father continues as the birds fade into the distance, "my father left more behind when he died than your mother's parents did. Turned out they had more pride than money. By the time their estate was settled, there was barely enough left over for a cemetery plot. My father at least left the cabin and a few bonds."

"You said your father changed the family name to Rose. Why?"

"Because of the discrimination he and my mother faced as

immigrants. He wanted a better life for me. 'Mining is not a living,' he'd say. 'It's a death.' He worked himself into an early grave sending me to college. He died of black lung before I finished graduate school. My mother died shortly after. Cancer, I think. She refused to see a doctor. Thought they were all quacks." He clears his throat. "I know you were upset when we sold the cabin, but you don't need old ghosts."

She detects the faintest note of bitterness in her father's voice, and she knows this is not easy for him to talk about. "What was the family name before it was changed to Rose?" Was it O'Rose, she wondered, or LaRose perhaps? Or something Eastern European, the giveaway syllables dropped?

"Are you sure we never told you? It was Rosa. My parents were Italian."

She is suddenly standing outside the Forum, the hot dust rising from the streets, and Raphael is buying her a rose. *To cheer you up. You are a Rosa, after all.*

"You all right?" she hears her father ask. "You look a little white. I shouldn't have told you these things. Would've been wiser to take the advice of that old proverb and leave them to lie like sleeping dogs. Probably why I never told you before."

"I'm okay," she says. "It's just that someone I once knew suggested I might be Italian. It's strange to find out after all this time that he was right."

"Fools rush in where angels fear to tread," her father mumbles as an apology, and she almost laughs. They would not get through this conversation without a quotation from Pope after all.

"No, really, I'm glad you told me all this. I wish you had before. It might have helped me understand you and Mom better."

"Were we that difficult? I know we probably had you too late in life. Too set in our ways. But I hoped you never doubted our love for you."

"Of course not," she says, deciding to follow the sleeping-dog proverb herself. Or maybe she is remembering the advice of Raphael. *Everything in your life has brought you to this point. Would you want it any different?* It's just that it was easier when she was lying next to him under the Tuscan sky. "I have often wished we related better, but we seem to be doing pretty well now. Perhaps we're just a family of late bloomers."

Her mother calls to them from the door, "Dinner is ready" echoing across the lake. "I hope Mom at least cooked some vegetables," Tulia says. "I worry about you two eating so much meat."

Her father hands her the book on his lap and gets up a little stiffly. "It would take more than a few rabbits to kill your mother and me. I just hope she brought some mead."

There is no mead, but a salad of wild greens brought from a health-food store in Pittsburgh sits on the table, and Tulia provides wine. They eat in the big room that serves as dining room, living room, and study. It has large windows that look out on mountains, lake, and the ginkgo sapling Tulia planted during her first summer here. Larger and brighter than the old cabin, this place with only a little work could be used all year round, something Tulia is contemplating. Strange she is becoming more reclusive than her parents ever thought of being. They had their work and each other, while she needs to make only occasional trips into the real world and has just a cat for company.

Mildred, already sated with handouts, yawns and curls up in the armchair that Tulia already thinks of as her father's. "Where did you get the name Mildred?" her mother asks, passing her the salad.

"I named her after the travel writer Mildred Mercy. Dad gave me her book before I went to Europe."

"Ah, yes, of course," he says, looking suspiciously at the contents of his plate. "A peculiar woman. Met her once. She gave a lecture at the library. I have the *Times* obituary in my files at home. Remind me to send it to you." He takes a bite of meat and nods his approval. "After the book was published, she returned to Tuscany and married a man twenty-five years her junior. A retired vintner, I believe. They were married for fifteen years. She died at age ninety-nine."

"She would have been eighty-four then when she married," Tulia says, remembering the man who rescued Miss Mercy in Arezzo and joking with Raphael about her knitting on the back of a scooter.

"I was very pleased when I found that book for you. It's very rare and quite possibly you have the last existing copy."

She feels contrite for having ever thought despairingly of his gift. As for the happy outcome of Miss Mercy's story, she can't help but be a little jealous, while all the time feeling guilty for begrudging the old woman her happiness.

Her mother has also made her own birthday cake, a heavy wholegrain loaf sweetened with honey and loaded with currants. They sing "Happy Birthday," and her mother blows out the single beeswax candle. She is delighted with Tulia's gift of cast-iron pots and is already planning to cook the entirety of the next day's meals in the fireplace. From her husband is a fat book on the history of food.

After dinner, Tulia insists on doing the dishes, and her parents take up their positions on either side of the fireplace. It is cooler now, and she lights the fire and finds her mother a sweater. Then she leaves them with Mildred and their books and goes down to the dock. Lying on her back, she looks up at the night sky. The kind of sky she thought of when looking into Raphael's eyes.

After almost two and a half years, the pain of losing him is beginning to dull, though learning about her Italian heritage, the talk of Miss Mercy, even this beautiful sky, have all conspired to bring the loss rushing back to her. She has stopped asking herself if it was worth it, those glorious few weeks in exchange for a lifetime of missing him. She knows now it was, that she would not change a thing—except the ending. And while he promised her she would understand one day, enlightenment still eludes her.

Shivering from the cool evening air, she gets up, ready to go back to the house. But at the end of the dock, she stops for a moment to enjoy the warm glow that radiates from the windows of her house. She loves this place and feels very fortunate to be here. Old friendships from her childhood have been rekindled and new ones made. She has enjoyed the summer parties and barbecues.

She remembers how she used to be intimidated by social situations and relied on Jasmine and then Ethan to be the life of the party for her as she stood in their shadows, feeling awkward. But now, finally, she is comfortable being herself, or this new version of herself. More confident, and yes, even a little happier than the pre-Raphael version.

Besides the people here, Mr. Sims in New York has taken to regularly inviting her over for dinner along with Tod, Tom, and the fiancée, and she also has become close to her editor, a woman her age who grew up in a small Vermont town and who was once as intimidated by the city as Tulia was. Tulia can laugh about that now, as she can about her dismal experiences at college.

Her mother appears at the window holding Mildred. Tulia waves although she knows her mother can't see her. She is glad she has made the effort to get to know her parents. Since her return from Europe, they have felt for the first time like a family. She has Raphael to thank for that.

With one last glance at the stars, she starts across the stretch of grass. Yes, her life has been blessed. The only thing that could make it better would be to open the door and find Raphael there, petting Mildred and talking to her parents. That warm smile with its hint of mischief. "There you are," he would say. "We were beginning to wonder where you were. Would you like some tea?" But she knows this will never happen, and when she opens the door, it is her mother asking if she wants tea.

"Thanks, that would be nice," she says.

Her mother hands her a recent edition of *The New York Times*. "Read this, then, while I make it."

New Raphael Painting Discovered

FLORENCE—Two years ago, Florentine art collectors Gaspare and Amelia Catania discovered a painting in the attic of their villa in the hills near Florence, Tuscany. The painting has been confirmed by experts as a lost work of the great Renaissance artist Raphael (also known as Raffaello Sanzio).

"We were cleaning out the attic and were shocked to discover the painting tucked away in a back corner," Ms. Catania said. The Catanias have chosen to donate the painting to the Uffizi Gallery in Florence. It will be put on temporary display at the Metropolitan Museum of Art in New York this fall.

The painting was transported to the Uffizi where it was put in the care of a team of archivists and preservers for extensive tests. At a press conference held yesterday, a spokesperson for the Uffizi described their efforts at identification: "We have considered whether a contemporary of Raphael's may have painted the portrait, perhaps one of his many students or assistants. But not even his best student, Giulio Romano, could capture the particular rhythms and delicacy of his master, and Raphael has long been considered virtually impossible to forge. The painting also includes the unique signature that the artist used on all paintings known to be done in his hand.

"We have every reason to believe this is a true Raphael, created during the last years of his life. We have of course considered the possibility of forgery. However, the carbon-fiber dating of the canvas and a close inspection of the paints themselves strongly suggest that it was indeed completed in Raphael's era. If it is the work of a modern forger, it is the work of a genius. Even the cracks in the paint are consistent with a painting of its age."

The painting is of a young woman. She has an expression on her face that has been described as more mysterious than Leonardo da Vinci's *Mona Lisa*. "Had this painting been known in its time, its fame might have even surpassed that of the *Mona Lisa,* said Westley Austin, an art historian from the University of Edinburgh and author of *Love Lives of the Artists.* Said Mr. Austin: "This previously unknown portrait casts doubt on the supposition that the subject of Raphael's 1518 painting, *La Fornarina,* was the love of Raphael's life."

Raphael was born in Urbino, Italy in 1483. He is widely considered to be one of the greatest painters of the Italian Renaissance, alongside Leonardo da Vinci and Michelangelo, and his work is said to most clearly express the harmony and balance of High Renaissance composition. He was one of the chief architects of St. Peter's as well as of several smaller churches in Rome, and he also designed hundreds of frescoes, paintings, and tapestries. In the last year of his life, he was made Director of Antiquities of Rome. He died suddenly of an unknown fever at age thirty-seven in 1520 and is buried in the Pantheon in Rome.

This story begins with the rain

Leaves of burgundy and yellow cling to dark branches, irides-cent against a darkening pewter sky. Tulia enters Central Park through the Artists' Gate. Holding a paper cup of hot tea that warms her cold fingers, she skirts by Wollman Rink and picks her way up the Mall, passing the angel that surmounts the Bethesda Fountain. Then, winding another loop of her scarf around her neck, she heads toward Fifth Avenue and the Metropolitan Museum of Art.

The invitation to the preview of the new Raffaello painting arrived the week after her parents' visit, and while it didn't specify, she assumes it is her book that earned her the honor. Whatever the reason, she is grateful to view the painting in relative quiet, since the Raffaello discovery is sure to bring out hordes of art students, schoolchildren, Renaissance aficionados, casual historians, and the public at large.

Even so, the display room bustles with Met members and other invited guests for the special viewing prior to the wine-and-cheese reception, and she must stand in line to shuffle past with everyone else. She is resigning herself to the wait, wishing she had checked her wool coat at the entrance, when she hears a voice behind her.

"Pretty exciting, wouldn't you say?"

She turns around and does a double take. "What are you doing here?"

He grins. "I'm so glad you remember me." He looks just as he did when she last saw him, though perhaps a little thinner. His hair is longer too, but his smile and enthusiasm are still the same.

"Of course I remember you, Matthew," she says, giving him a hug. "Where's Caroline?" She scans the line behind him for his wife.

"Unfortunately, we're no longer together. She lives in Montreal now."

"I'm so sorry to hear that. You two seemed so happy in Venice."

He shakes his head. "That's why we were there, trying to work things out. But even Venice couldn't save us." He smiles. "We're still friends though." He seems relaxed about it, as if he has made his peace with the situation. "I read *For My Beloved*. I really liked it. You seemed rather unsure of yourself when you were working on it in Venice, but obviously you knew what you were doing."

"Thank you," she says. "And thanks for your encouragement. It came at a crucial time." He'll never know how the story of him and Caroline meeting in Paris prompted her to forgive Raphael. "Are you in New York on vacation?"

"Actually, I moved here from Toronto this past summer. I've joined the faculty at NYU."

She welcomes him to New York, and their section of the line is finally allowed to enter the chamber. She can see the painting on the opposite side, a dark splotch on the white wall, the security guards stationed on either side, the velvet rope keeping viewers, three people deep, well away from the priceless work. Strangely, she feels almost nervous. Trying not to look, wanting to see the painting for the first time up close, she tries to focus on her conversation with Matthew: memories of Venice, his new job, her apartment in the city and house in the Poconos.

Finally she is in front of it, and she allows herself to look.

It may have been lost, but she knows this painting. The rolling green hills dotted with red poppies. The resplendent blue skies. And she knows this woman. Those lips that hint at laughter, the reason for the smile. And she knows those blue eyes, a dusky version of the sky, and every dream and desire behind them. She knows too the white gown trimmed with lace, the feel of the gauzy shawl draped over one arm. She closes her eyes, so confused she doesn't know whether to laugh or cry.

How will I know they're yours?

You will know.

She knows too the villa where it was found. The garden where it was painted. And the touch of the artist's lips on hers. A con artist after all. She can take comfort that she is not the only one he fooled, for he has fooled the best. Carbon-daters, scholars, and all.

The same painting done in chalk on the sidewalk in Rome. *Is this a copy of the painting you made of me at the villa? I wish you would let me see the original.*

And his evasive response. *I hope one day.*

A Raffaello indeed.

"Are you all right?" It is Matthew, grasping her elbow. She opens her eyes and, avoiding the painting, looks at him. "It is an incredible work," he says, as if that explains her reaction. "And it truly does outshine the *Mona Lisa.* For not only is there the mystery of her smile, there's the element of grace that is so unmistakably and uniquely Raphael's. All the women he painted were beautiful, and yet this one is different. One can see from looking at it that he had truly met his muse . . ." Matthew breaks off, looking from the painting to Tulia. "Oh my," he says. "No wonder you're so pale. It looks just like *you.*"

Should she tell him? Surely this is going to go down in art-fraud history. She wishes she hadn't played a role in it, even if an innocent one. But where to start?

She looks back at the painting. It is certainly a flattering portrait, every bit as perfect as if Raffaello himself had painted it. Every unruly curl as her hair cascades over her shoulder acquiring an elegance she did not know it possessed.

"What's that in her hair?" Matthew asks. And she sees it at the same time. The painting is small, no larger than the *Mona Lisa,* so it is easy enough to miss. But already she knows. With a glance at the bored-looking security guards, she steps as close as the rope will allow her.

"What is it?" Matthew asks eagerly.

"A comb," she whispers. And so she is wrong about Raphael again. For she never told him about the comb. Nor could he have learned it from her book, published after the painting's discovery. The comb of her dreams, made of gold and inlaid with three rubies. The comb belonging to Raffaello's beloved. The comb she threw away the day Raffaello died, when she wished that she too might die.

Not a forgery—but the truth even more impossible.

The same painting done in chalk on the sidewalk in Rome. Only in this painting she wears a comb.

She stands at the rope, Matthew behind her, and the line moves around them. She hears a whispered voice behind her. "Isn't that the woman who wrote *For My Beloved?*" Do they notice the painting looks just like her? Perhaps her wool coat is sufficient disguise. Or is it her bewildered expression? So different from the dreamy eyes of her portrait.

"What do you think she's looking at?" Matthew asks.

Tulia meets the beguiling eyes of the woman in the painting. *Her* eyes. "She's looking at Raphael," she says, finally finding her voice, knowing Matthew won't distinguish which Raphael she's referring to.

"And what is she thinking?"

A heartbeat. "She's wondering if she loves him." She is carried back to the luxuriant Tuscan landscape, Raphael at his easel, the scent of flowers in the garden, the droning bees and singing birds, the warm wine and dream-infused sun, the dizzying realization of being on the cusp of love. How is any of this possible?

Matthew stares at her, then begins to recite:

> "Less of the heavens, and more of earth,
> There lurk within these earnest eyes
> The passions that have had their birth
> And grown beneath Italian skies."

"William Allen Butler," he says. "'Incognita of Raphael.'" She doesn't respond. She knows this verse. The epigraph of her book. "And does she? Love him that is?"

She remembers another line from the poem. *Not soon shall I forget the day, sweet day, in spring's unclouded time.* "Yes," she says simply.

"You seem quite sure."

"I am." Could it be? Could it really be possible? Her dream not a dream but a memory. A memory of another place, another time, another life. No wonder the dream used to frighten and sadden her. It was the pain of real grief, of realizing she had lost the man she loved so completely, of knowing her life would be changed irrevocably.

And her book—their story remembered, made real. No longer lost to history, resurrected . . .

I promise one day you will understand.

"Are you ready?" Matthew says as the crowd presses up behind them. Tulia, almost powerless to tear herself away from the painting, leans on his arm and lets him guide her toward the noisy reception hall.

But in the lobby, she stops. She cannot go in. She needs quiet, she needs to think, she needs time to figure all this out. "Thank you, Matthew. But I have to go." And she hastens toward the exit, leaving him standing there, not even asking for his phone number.

Once outside, she hesitates. A group of smokers are gathered around the entrance, and their laughter comes to her from far away. Taxis honk as they whisk down Fifth Avenue. She pulls her coat around her to ward off the damp wind, each gust a reminder of where she is. I am in New York, she thinks, compelled to rhyme off these certainties as she starts down the steps. *My name is Tulia Rose, although my family name was once Rosa. Tulia is from the Latin, meaning strong rain. I am twenty-seven years old. I am a writer* . . .

On the bottom step she sits down, not sure what to do next, not sure what to believe. A blast of wind catches the leaves on the sidewalk, and they rise like a flock of birds, swirling among the pedestrians like the fat pigeons in the Piazza San Marco.

. . . I am a writer, and once I knew a painter named Raphael. She raises her eyes to the sky, a mélange of dying orange sun and gray clouds, rich as a sky chalked on a sidewalk in Paris.

Raphael. Pulling poppies from his sleeve. *I was beginning to think you were not coming,* he said. The story of a woman in a marketplace, buying oranges. He never stopped loving her. But they had been separated from each other for a very long time. And the story of an angel. Painted in chalk in a quiet park in Venice. And a woman in a church who wore a golden comb. Reminding her of the comb from her dreams. The archangel, patron saint of lovers, of healing, of happy meetings, of happy endings. *If there was only one happy ending, life would get a little dull. Sort of like heaven.* And in the flourishing garden of a Tuscan villa, when time stood still and a painting was kept secret. Knowing the stories that no historian knew. Helping her write their story. And dreams of a dying artist in Rome. Her own heart breaking. Kissing under an umbrella on the Sant'Angelo Bridge. *I love you,* he said as the rain fell. And when she opened her eyes, he was gone.

The rain always knew the story of Raphael.

Her Raphael. Painter. Painter of angels. Guardian angel. Her angel.

She understands now, as unbelievable as it seems. He could not stay forever. *God knows how much I have prayed,* he said. *But it is impossible.* However, this time not leaving without painting her, without telling her how he feels. Not making the same mistake twice.

Her Raffaello. Her Raffaele. Her Raphael.

You just have to close your eyes and dream. Eyes so dark she could see the edge of heaven. And herself reflected back from somewhere in time. She knows now she has always been there. And always will be. That is the way their story goes.

When she opens her eyes, Matthew is sitting quietly beside her on the step. "Are you all right?" he asks, a worried expression lining his face. "You left in such a hurry."

"I'm sorry," she says. "I had to get away. It was all so . . . overwhelming." She is glad to have him by her side, rooting her to this world, the New World, where she was born and lives.

"It's very powerful," he says. "And it must have been a shock, to see yourself looking back from a sixteenth-century portrait. It's uncanny."

If I told you, it would not be magic.

She smiles. "You could say that."

Only a trickle of people exit or enter the Met; the reception must be in full swing. Even most of the smokers have disappeared, perhaps to hear the keynote speaker, an art specialist flown in from the University of Venice. He will not, however, know the whole story.

"When you were in Venice," she asks as something new occurs to her, "did you go into the Chiesa dell'Angelo Raffaele?"

He looks puzzled. "No, it's been closed for restoration for years. I think it's still closed."

"So the paintings wouldn't have been there then?"

He shakes his head. "Why?"

"Just wondering." She doesn't tell him that one morning two years ago the church was open and the paintings of the archangel were there.

"Are you working on another novel?" Matthew asks.

"Yes, on Petrarch and Laura. I hope to be finished in early spring."

"So it's coming along well."

"It is, but I'm already looking forward to my next book. It's going to be based on my grandfather who was a miner in Pennsylvania." She has known for a while that she will set her next novel in the Poconos, but this is her first realization that it will stem from her father's family history.

"No more writer's block then," Matthew says, smiling.

"No. If anything, the opposite. I can barely keep up with my ideas."

"I look forward to reading them both." He takes a deep breath, looking slightly nervous. "Would you like to go for a cup of coffee, Tulia?"

Promise me you will concentrate on the new stories.

I will try, Raphael.

"That would be lovely, Matthew."

"I have a confession," he says, getting up and holding his hand out to her. "I saw in the newspaper that you were an invited guest. I came here specifically to find you. I hope you don't mind." His hand is warm in hers, and she is aware of how real he feels. "I've been trying to get up the nerve to contact you ever since I moved to New York."

"I'm glad you did."

They walk along the sidewalk where the street vendors are packing away their wares for the night. At an entrance to Central Park, they pass a cart overflowing with fragrant flowers—purple mums, white roses, red poppies.

"How unusual to see poppies this time of year," Matthew says with delight, and he reaches for his wallet to buy her one.

A light rain begins to fall, and she lifts her face to the sky.

This sprinkle of rain like a blessing.

Matthew hands Tulia the delicate bloom, then opens his umbrella over them as they walk together down Fifth Avenue.

Epilogue

From the roof of the Met, silhouetted against the last flush of dusk, he watches. Watches until their umbrella is so small, he can no longer make it out in the November gloom. He drops the remains of his cigarette on the rooftop, where it glows for a moment before sputtering out. The rain falls steadily now, turning to silver in the headlights of cars and taxis, while snippets of conversation float up to him from the steps below. Who was she? . . . surely Raphael's lover . . . so beautiful . . .

A dove, dragging one twisted wing, flounders along the edge of the roof. He picks it up, pulling a wet leaf from its feathers. The bird nestles against his vest, dry despite the rain, its embroidered tangle of flowers and birds and suns like the memory of summer.

"Heaven," he whispers to the bird, "drives a hard bargain." But he should not complain. That night in Roma, burning up with fever, he had raged against God. Why now? At least let me tell her . . . And had not his prayers been answered? Had he not been given that second chance? To help her, to paint her, to love her. But such was the agreement that he had to leave her the moment he said those words. I love you.

He knows it will never be over for him. But at least now, having told her how he feels, he can find some peace at last. Holding out the bird, he kisses it gently on the head and watches it fly away. Soft white wings on the velvet of night. Then looking out over the darkened, rain-drenched streets to the spot where he saw her last, he murmurs, as he does every night, "Good night, Tulia, my beloved."

Acknowledgments

S pecial thank-yous to Elizabeth Greene for her unwavering
faith in us and *The Sidewalk Artist;* to John Pearce, our wonderful agent; and to our editor, Peter Joseph, for being such a pleasure
to work with.

To those who read drafts, offered technical advice and help,
or otherwise encouraged or inspired us: Ajay and Amelia
Agrawal; Christine, Krishna, and Aneil Agrawal; Tony, Lydia, and
Andy Buonaguro; Mary Cameron; David Chown; Mike Clark;
Westley and Austin Côté; Frances Daunt; Camille DeSimone;
Erica Garrington; James Gregor; Steven Heighton; Brian
Henry; Gaspare Ingoglia; Janice's colleagues in "Honolulu"; Tara
Kainer; Allen, Doris, and Lori Kirk; David Macfarlane; Lisa
McHale; Gabrielle McIntire; Robert Meddows-Taylor; Chris
Miner; Keyvan and Bahereh Hastrudi-Zaad; Emily, Pamela,
and Susan Neal; Kim Ondaatje; Jessica Papin; Mary Pasterello;
Gail Pearce; Cecil Perido; Susanne Peterson; Kris Quinlan; the
real Raphael; Rosemount Inn; Krys Ross; Alexander, Gail, and

Clelia Scala; Heather Spragins; the staff at St. Martin's Press; Jennifer Thaler; Archbishop Desmond Tutu; the staff at Westwood Creative Artists; Sunita Wiebe; and others too numerous to list here—thank you.